Backbone of the King

Backbone of the King

THE STORY OF PAKA'A AND HIS SON KU

by Marcia Brown

A KOLOWALU BOOK
University of Hawaii Press
Honolulu

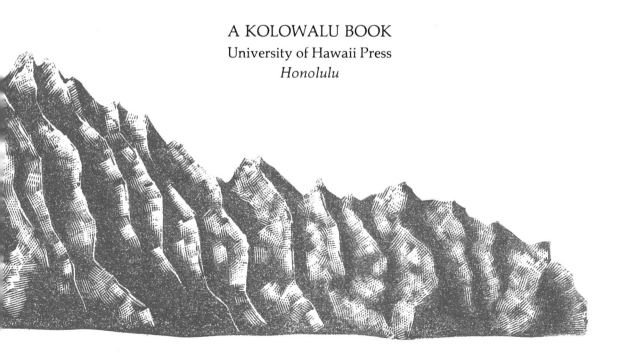

Printed in the United States of America

This story is based on *The Hawaiian Story of Pakaa
and Kuapakaa, the Personal Attendants of
Keawenuiaumi* . . . , collected, assembled, selected, and edited by
Moses K. Nakuina. Honolulu, n.d.

Translation from the Hawaiian by Dorothy M. Kahananui

TO ESTHER

"The burden of the hands is the paddle;
  The fighter of the waves is the paddle.
  I leave the black one for you,
  I take the white one for me.
  Dip the paddle, turn up the foam,
  On the inside, on the outside,
  On the outside, on the inside.
  The canoe throbs ahead . . ."

CHAPTER ONE

They called him Paka'a, but who could tell how the
boy had got such an odd name?

The people of the village were used to seeing him, the
proud and silent child, standing at the edge of the taro
patch, watching with a thoughtful expression the men plant
in water the tender plant tops. The child watched, and then
strode away, shaking his head. Not for him that backbreak-
ing work in the mud.

9

Paka'a was there, running with the hunters through the scrub trees of the uplands after the wild boar. But when the beast stopped, squealing, caught in the meshes of the throwing net, he made no move to throw even one stone with the others.

He was there on the beach, daring to play in the sea with the children of high caste. Paka'a was big and strong. Already he could keep his balance on his small koa board and ride a wave into shore. By his skill alone he won his right to sport with nobles.

"But he's a nothing—the son of an unknown, and a slave," the people said. And who did know anything about the father of Paka'a, except that he had landed one day at Kapa'a on the coast of Kaua'i, a wanderer without rank? He had worked as well as any man, thatching his house with the hala that grew so plentifully. He paddled his canoe like a master, he surfed like a gannet swooping over the waves. But—who knew of his family, of his fathers? Where were his lands? What was his place?

The stranger had won to wife the beautiful La'amaomao, daughter of a priestly family. They had wished for a better match for their daughter, one that would bring lands and wealth—a marriage to a high chief. They did not take to the choice of their daughter's heart. The man built his wife's house next to his own, and there the couple went to live.

And then one day a messenger had come from far off, and the tall stranger had gone, had left his young wife, and was soon forgotten. Aloha! Auwe! Island people get used to farewells.

In time a little son was born to Laʻamaomao. Her parents closed their home to the mother and her baby; so she went to live on the pali that rises above the sea near Kapaʻa, and there she brought up the boy.

One alone of her family loved her—Maʻilou the birdhunter. His little sister had been his favorite from the time when he was a child and carried the fat little girl everywhere on his back. It was he who taught her the figures of the string game, and she sat on his lap to swing over the ravine from the strong koali vine. She was still his favorite.

So when Ma'ilou saw that his parents would have nothing to do with his sister, he went to live with her and help bring up her child. To a Hawaiian, a child is a good to be shared; to Paka'a, Ma'ilou was father. And so the village soon thought of him too.

Ma'ilou was an expert bird-hunter, but it took many little birds to feed three people. So the child would run down to the beach where the canoes set out for the deep water. He would watch the canoes, so tiny from the shore, form the splashing crescent that would drive the fish into the bag nets. He would still be there on the beach when the men brought in the glistening catch. Some people would give the boy a few fish, enough for a meal. But others would say, "Why don't you fish for birds—with your father?" And Paka'a would hang his head. He took the fish, but— he wondered.

In the morning Paka'a looked at Ma'ilou as he set out at dawn. Small of bone and agile, he easily climbed the hillside, pulling down the branches to help himself spring higher. Paka'a looked down at his own body, muscular and large-boned for a boy his age. He would be a tall man.

He ran to his mother's house.

"Who is my father?"

La'amaomao stepped out of the dark of the hut. "Why, there on the hill, Ma'ilou. There goes your father." She did not want to tell the boy yet of his father's going.

"No. Ma'ilou is small. I am large. He cannot be my father."

La'amaomao knew the time had come to tell the boy the truth.

"How you pester me! Ma'ilou is your father because he cares for you like one. He is my own brother. But your father who gave you life, him you have not seen. Look to the east where the sun rises. Look there, from where the trade winds blow. There, far off to the east, there dwells your father."

The boy fell silent. He looked up at the great rosy mounds of the dawn clouds pushed by the eastern winds, rushing, rushing over his head. He shivered. He was small after all; he had no canoe. He could not paddle the broad blue waters between the islands. But when he could, he would go and seek his father.

Meanwhile there was growing to do, and watching, and by watching, learning—to farm the taro, to hunt the wild duck, to carve with an adz, to fish; and there was playing—a great deal of playing.

Of all the work he saw, Paka'a liked fishing the best. Being on the water might carry him closer to that distant father. Day after day he watched canoes go out to sea and return with the malolo.

"E ku'u makuahine," he said to La'amaomao, "why do we have so little when those others eat often and much?"

"Because your uncle would rather hunt birds than fish. He is limber and good at mountain-climbing. It is his work."

"Then can't I go fishing? Perhaps I'd get a share of the catch."

"But how can you go fishing when you can't even swim? You could drown."

"While you have been busy, I have gone swimming with the other children. You don't have to worry about my drowning. When Ma'ilou returns, would you ask him to carry the canoe he was paddling the other morning down to the water's edge for me?"

"What a nagger you are. Well, we'll see what you can do." La'amaomao smiled.

All those mornings waiting on the shore Paka'a had seen the malolo fishermen paddle far out beyond the reef to the deep water. When they could scarcely see the mountains any more, there they found the flying fish. And when they returned Paka'a saw how tired they were from the long paddle back.

There must be an easier way. He decided to prepare himself. First he cut two straight sticks almost twice his height. Then, from some rolls of split lauhala that his mother had been using for weaving mats, he wove a small, squarish mat. He tied two corners to the two ends of one stick and one side to the other stick.

That evening, after they had finished their meal of broiled birds, La'amaomao called over to Ma'ilou, sitting in the doorway of his house.

"E Ma'ilou...tomorrow, don't hurry off too early to the hills, but you two lift your old canoe down to the beach for the boy. He has been pestering me to go fish malolo."

"The boy eats flesh that I catch, and malolo that the neighbors give him. Doesn't he get enough, that he begs to go fishing?"

Paka'a spoke up. "Don't keep me from going. I'll fish for *us*. We won't have to eat other people's bait fish."

Ma'ilou smarted at that. "We will not hold you. Tomorrow you shall go."

That evening, by the light of the afterglow, Ma'ilou and Paka'a lifted the canoe down to the beach—a little apart from the others. In the morning Paka'a took his water gourd, his bag, the sticks, and the mat.

"What are the sticks for? Why are you taking the mat?" Ma'ilou was amazed.

"One question at a time. The sand crab is small but digs a deep hole." Paka'a grinned at his uncle.

"But here you go fishing with two sticks and a mat. What a laugh!"

"You fish with the wrong hook. This stick is a mast for my canoe, and this one is a boom to hold out my sail, this mat. You know how far out to sea the flying fish go. When we catch the fish and are about to return, I shall set up my mast and sail, like this. When the cool Kapa'a wind blows, I'll steer with my paddle. You'll see whose shoulders won't be weary. Now do you understand?"

Ma'ilou did understand. He looked at the boy, so sure of himself, and he thought of the tall stranger who had married his own sister.

"Yes—and one day people will tell of how you put a stop to aching shoulders with your canoe. Let it sail!"

So he and the boy gave a push, Paka'a jumped in, caught up the paddle; and as Ma'ilou looked, it seemed the boy was already a master. He paddled with no splashes, and the canoe leaped ahead, alive, over the water.

The men in the malolo fleet cried out, "Auwe noho'i e! Here comes La'amaomao's son all alone in a canoe! Where's his father?"

"Fishing for birds!" They laughed.

Soon they reached the place where the malolo jumped ahead of them. The lead fisherman called for them to line up their canoes abreast of each other, and the drive of the malolo began.

Paka'a's canoe was in the middle of the fleet, but when he saw that the men at the outside edges reached the canoes holding the corners of the net and got fish before the others, he stopped paddling and held back until the other canoes closed in. Then he quickly darted his small canoe to the outside, near the corner canoe.

The older fishermen shouted and tried to block his way, but Paka'a did not listen. He caught hold of the cords, lifted the edge of the net; and when the school of fish was surrounded, he was able to scoop eighty fish into his canoe.

When they were all ready to return, Paka'a challenged the fishermen. "Who will race with me and let our fish be the stake?"

A huge man alone in a canoe accepted. But Paka'a asked, "How many malolo have you?"

"Eight fish."

"That's not enough for a wager."

"How many fish have you then?"

"Two ka'au—eighty."

When the men in another canoe overheard this, they called out, "Let's wager. You seem to want a lot of fish! There are eight of us. With ten fish each for us, we can equal yours."

"That's up to you," said Paka'a. "I'm ready."

"We challenge you."

"Agreed, but give me your fish."

"But we should hold our fish and yours."

"No. You can see I'm a small boy. I've not even put on a malo. You are eight strong men. If you beat me, it will be easy enough for you to get my fish. But if I should beat you, you might not give up yours."

"He's right. Do what he says."

So Paka'a paddled his canoe close to the large canoe, and the men scooped all their fish into his.

"The canoe that touches dry land first wins!"

When all was ready, a man in another canoe stood to line them up. When they were even, he chanted:

> "Stand, stand, island ruler,
> Get set.
> 'Oia! Right!"

When he said, " 'Oia!" the men in the large canoe started to paddle and dashed off, while Paka'a dawdled at the rear. When they were quite some distance away, he nosed his bow to the wind and set up his mast and sail. The others turned back to look.

"Look at him wasting time. He isn't even coming."

"What an odd fellow!"

"What's that sticking up?"

"It's a stick with a mat. Now why...?"

They called out, "Lateness and an empty bag are what you will get out of this wager, young upstart!"

Paka'a didn't answer but turned his canoe toward land. The wind blew astern, the sail swelled ahead, and the canoe began to skim over the water. The boy set his paddle fast to steer and leaned back. He felt the wind with him and chanted:

"Blow, wind of Ukoa.
See the bow dash along,
Cuffed about by the wind.
Leave the friends at Puna.
This is being borne along,
Borne along by the water."

When the men in the large canoe looked again, they saw Paka'a sailing swiftly toward them, crowding in behind them, right on their tail.

"Here comes that boy—ho! Here he comes with that big thing billowing. He sits, he does not paddle. We are the ones that are working!"

Paka'a's canoe passed the big canoe; the men strained at their paddles, but no use. The light canoe sped to its goal. Paka'a grinned at the men's bent shoulders, and called:

> "Drink the water of the ghosts!
> Straight to the shore
> Sails the over-burdened.
> It has landed,
> The helmsman has landed.
> O men who risk your fish—
> Life-food of priests—land!
> Strive to beach your canoe.
> The first-born child eats the season's
>   first malolo."

The taunts angered the men, but Paka'a paid no heed. In no time at all he had landed on the shore. The race was his.

From the shore the people had seen. "That billowy thing on the sea. Say! That billowy thing on the sea—there!" And because it headed for the landing place, they headed there too. Then they saw that it was a small canoe with a mast and sail, and in it was Paka'a, La'amaomao's child.

21

They crowded around, they praised Paka'a, they helped him lift his canoe to the dry land as if he were a relative. To each who helped, Paka'a gave malolo. Then he took down the mast, rolled up the sail, put the fish in his lauhala bag, and went home.

"Here's our fish, Mother. I had two ka'au of malolo. Then I raced with eight men and won theirs too. I gave some away to the people who helped me beach my canoe."

When La'amaomao saw the fish and heard the story, she was proud. "Bringing you up is a strong tree planted. You will bring life to my bones."

Ma'ilou put aside the birds he had caught. "Tonight we eat malolo." Eat they did until they were full. And it was Paka'a who offered fish to the neighbors.

CHAPTER TWO

At that time Pai'ea was chief of Kaua'i, a high chief, descended from kings. One day he took it into his head to tour all the islands in the group; so he sent for his kahuna and soothsayers to find out when to start. They noted the cloud-omens and reported that the way was clear, but that it would be good to tour his own island first.

News of the king's tour raced around the island. People prepared poi and fish and gifts of fine kapa for the day when the king would arrive with his court. For many would go with him on his tour, some as honored retainers, some as invited guests, and some as slaves.

When the news reached Kapa'a, Paka'a saw the villagers wrapping bundles and trying to wangle a place on the tour.

"Why do you make up those bundles?" he asked.

"We want to go on tour with Pai'ea, our chief. He will first tour Kaua'i, and after that O'ahu and Maui, and finally go far, far off, to Hawai'i."

"Where are those places? Are they far from here? Are they to the east?"

"We cannot see those islands . . ."

"Then I would go with the chief."

"That's up to you."

Paka'a ran home to tell La'amaomao this news. "Mother, I will go on tour with Pai'ea. Say I may?"

His mother did not answer immediately, but was thoughtful. Then she spoke. "You may be ill-treated and ordered around as if you were a slave." She knew that a

23

slave was often of no more value than a pig or a fish when a sacrifice was to be made.

"Mother, since when were saying 'yes,' listening, and being asked to do things ill-treatment? I can fetch water and do other little things children do, and what I cannot do can be done by a grown-up person."

The boy's reply was humble. La'amaomao gave her consent.

So Paka'a went on the tour, not as a retainer, certainly not invited, but tagging along as an errand boy. The people in the chief's retinue ordered him here, shouted him there; but when they divided the chief's gifts, they never thought of a share for him. During all this, the boy was patient. Paka'a had an idea. Right now it was enough to learn the ways of a court.

But on that tour of Pai'ea, who really wanted for food? "Stuff when food is in the hand. Traveling with the king is a whale-tooth necklace..." the people said. They ate to burst, and wasted as much as they ate. Paka'a managed to fill his stomach. The commoners of Kaua'i had been lavish in gifts to their chief.

So the tour went, with games and gift ceremonies and sham fights by day, and feasting and dancing and chanting by night. At the edge of the crowd, near the drummer, crouched a bright-eyed boy, listening, and watching, and remembering. Later on he would escape to the forest to chant to himself what he had heard. Thus Paka'a learned and memorized the stories and chants of his island.

The high chief Pai'ea visited all the famous places of Kaua'i, from Waimea of the reddish water to mist-hung Ha'ena. When the tour was finished, Paka'a went back to Kapa'a.

Not long after that, the tour to the other islands was announced. The boy had been useful on the Kaua'i tour. He would be useful again, more useful, because he had learned much. He went to his mother.

"You, my mother, who have brought me up alone, cut off from your fathers, please let me go with Pai'ea the chief to O'ahu. Perhaps he will go to Hawai'i. Perhaps—if he lives—I shall see my father."

"Yes, go," said his mother, "but go in meekness. Listen carefully, do all you are asked to do. Be patient until you arrive at Hawai'i. At the pali of Waipi'o, there dwells your father. If it is said that you have arrived at the place of Keawe-nui-a-'Umi, then say to yourself you have at last reached the place of your father.

"At the court, you will see two old, gray-haired men. He who wears a feather mantle and a whale-tooth necklace around his neck and carries a fan in his hand is your master, Keawe-nui-a-'Umi. He who holds the kahili, the high feather standard of royalty, he is Ku-a-Nu'uanu, your father. Do not doubt. Do not be afraid. But go sit on his lap, as only a true son may. Let him ask your name. Tell him your name, Paka'a, named with love after his master's skin, cracked from drinking 'awa. Your father will know you for his son. Life, honor, and wealth will be yours. No more will worthless people order you about. Your father is a chief of Hawai'i and the kahu iwikuamo'o, the backbone of the king."

When La'amaomao had finished speaking, she took the lid off a large calabash and took out a small whistling gourd, smoothly encased in woven 'ie'ie and having a small cover of its own.

Turning to her son, she said, "I give you this calabash, which belonged to your grandmother, whose name I bear. In it are her bones and all the winds of the islands that were her slaves:

> The strong wind that jerks bait off the line,
> The thirsty wind called Drink-water,
> The raging sea-wind called Heap of Violence,
> The high wind tied to heaven,
> The calm wind called Broad-leaf . . .

"Before she died she asked me to put her bones in this calabash and guard them well until I should have a child. Now I give to you the wind calabash of La'amaomao. Guard it well. You cannot know its true value yet.

"But when you voyage with your chief and are becalmed, call and the wind will blow.

"If people taunt you, lift the lid slightly and call. The clean wind will clear the air, and bear you and your canoes to land. Your chief will honor you.

"The calabash is yours. Use it only when you need it."

Paka'a looked at his mother with awe; and as she gazed back at him, calm and strong, he felt in her the mana, the power of his grandmother over wind and storm. And Paka'a knew now who he was, son of an ali'i, highest of chiefs but for the king, and named with love.

But time was short. There was much to learn before Paka'a was to sail. Day after day, while others prepared the bundles of food and kapas for the trip, La'amaomao spent time with the boy, teaching him the names of all the winds, the prayers and meles to call them forth.

When Paka'a had memorized them all, he tied the wind calabash in a net with his supplies. He was ready to go. From a corner in her house his mother brought forth a bundle.

"This kapa, this mantle, this malo, are for you to put on when you go to meet your father. He left them for you. Go now, and don't look back."

And so the shaft that ten years before had entered the heart of La'amaomao was sped back to its sender. Aloha!

That day of departure, so many chiefs and followers went along with Pai'ea that the winds over the channel were calmed by the cloud of canoes spread over the waters.

Pai'ea and his followers landed at Waikiki and were entertained by the chiefs of O'ahu. After a few days, they sailed on to Moloka'i and then to Maui. Finally they reached Kohala on the island of Hawai'i. When the people saw the cloud of canoes, even though the strokes of the paddles were not muffled for surprise, they feared war. They made ready to fight.

But when the scouts arrived and saw that it was Pai'ea of Kaua'i, come as friend, their fear died, and they welcomed him as a high chief. Messengers arrived from the king, Keawe-nui-a-'Umi, to conduct him to the court at Waipi'o.

Many of the retainers and courtiers went by overland
trail. Pai'ea, the high chief, sailed to Waipi'o in his double
canoe, sailed with his gods fixed before him and the bright
kapa streamer floating from the high mast, sailed around
the toothed pali of Waipi'o, framed by the green cliffs
against the blue sky.

There on the shore waited Keawe-nui-a-'Umi in his mantle of golden feathers, with his guards and attendants and priests, to greet the visitors. *That* welcome was royal.

The greeting was warm. The people of the valley had brought food—hundreds of pigs, dogs, chickens, wild ducks, bananas, and taro—so much food that some said,

"If we reach down our throats, the food has stuck!" On that first day of the visit of Pai'ea the smokes from the imu roasting the gift food blacked out the sun.

And that is how it was until all the food was eaten and the flow of gifts dried up. Then the stomachs pinched. Those who could, made friends with natives who ate; the others starved.

So it always was. At first, welcome and gifts and feasting. Then you were looked on as a native and could fend for yourself. The feast-mat had worn thin.

In the first days of Pai'ea's visit, Paka'a had looked for his father. From where he stood in the crowd of natives he saw, far off, the royal enclosure, the pa, with the guards and soldiers at the gate. He caught a glimpse of the king in his feather mantle, sitting on a platform, and by his side a tall, white-haired man holding the red kahili of the king.

"O my mother, I remember!" Paka'a knew his good fortune, but he could wait his chance to speak.

Meanwhile famine bent the backs of Pai'ea's followers. While the natives stuffed and the odors from their imu floated over the valley, Paka'a and the others blinked their eyes and their mouths watered.

One day Paka'a stood up and looked around at the hungry courtiers. He decided he must act.

"That food over there." He pointed toward a large imu not far from the royal enclosure. "If I can go before those old men, it can be mine."

"Young upstart! Don't you know who they are? The king of Hawai'i is a high kapu chief. Don't you see the guards? Don't you know that the shadow that runs before you on the ground can bring you death?"

"If I can get to see them, I'll get food, and we shall live."

"How can a worthless one get food when Pai'ea goes hungry?" The men turned their backs on the boy.

He who serves learns patience. Paka'a did not reply for a moment. Ahead might lie death, but to do nothing meant starvation. Already, grown men were weakening. He spoke.

"This body will be bait. The king must learn how it is with us. You will live and return to our island."

The boy unwrapped the bundle of kapa given him by his mother. For the first time he put on the pure white malo, the mantle, the blanket of finest gauze. When all was ready he took a fan in his hand and stepped out in front of the others, no longer the slave, the worthless one, but the child of a chief, without fear.

Before the men could say anything, he was off, lost in the crowd of natives. Then they caught a flash of white near the gate; then they lost sight of it. But in a moment they heard the cries.

"That child violates the sacred place of the king! Auwe! The child breaks the kapu!" There was a great stir of guards rushing toward the king and the kahili bearer.

For Paka'a had found a gap in the line of guards when one had turned to speak to another. The boy darted through, edged past the pulo'ulo'u, the white kapa ball that marked the kapu, and before anyone could catch him, ran up to the king, grabbed the kahili which Ku-a-Nu'uanu was holding, and leaped onto the lap of his father.

"Auwe! Ke keiki! Ke kapu!"

Ku-a-Nu'uanu drew back in anger, but Paka'a was quick. He saw that his father meant to let him fall between his legs; so he threw his right leg over his father's right thigh and clung there, astride.

Ku-a-Nu'uanu had lifted his arm to brush the boy off his leg like an insect. Suddenly he thought: Only a true son may sit on a father's lap. He made a sign for the guards to wait before they struck.

"Whose child are you?"

"I am the child of Ku-a-Nu'uanu and La'amaomao." The father saw the pure white malo of fine kapa.

"Are you Paka'a?"

"'Ae. I am Paka'a."

"You are Paka'a after whom?"

"After Keawe-nui-a-'Umi, named with love for his cracked skin."

Aloha flooded the father's heart. "Then you are indeed my child." He gathered the boy to himself, rubbed the small nose with his large one, and wept in a loud voice, wept for the love lost and left behind, wept for relief for the lost now found, wept for joy. All ears heard the cry of that weeping.

34

The king asked, "Whose child is this?"

"This is my own child, blood of my blood," said Ku-a-Nu'uanu, "who was not yet born when your messenger called me back from my trip to Kaua'i. My bones were yours. I left with his mother his name, his name after you, after the rough look of your skin. O my king!"

"Your trip was blessed. I shall have a new attendant."
The king was pleased with Paka'a. "Teach him all there is
to know concerning your duties. Do not overlook a single
thing. If you should go the narrow stranded way before me,
he can care for me."

"O my king! I will dig deep!"

While the heart of Keawe-nui-a-'Umi went out to both
father and son, the heart of Ku-a-Nu'uanu was full to
bursting. Great gifts that day!

The king sent his messengers among his people to
bring food and gift offerings to Paka'a, son of Ku-a-
Nu'uanu, his new attendant. The messengers raced through
the countryside, and all the people, Pai'ea and all his followers, all those who had ridiculed and made a slave of
Paka'a, all heard the news. And these last ones wondered
and whispered among themselves. What would be their
fate? They feared for their lives.

But Paka'a bore them no ill will. For many months he
had been learning patience with men. He remembered again
his mother's words, "Go in meekness . . ."

So that day there were two huge fires and two columns
of imu smoke reached to the sky; the people made two
presentations of gifts, one to Paka'a and one to Pai'ea. For
when the natives of Waipi'o brought their offerings, Paka'a
ordered them to give most of them to Pai'ea and his companions from Kaua'i, to each according to his rank.

And that night the pahu hula boomed and the knee
drums crackled; the bamboo pipes rang, and the chant rose

through the night to Laka, goddess of the dance. The king drank 'awa, and 'awa was offered to the high chiefs.

After the 'awa and the hulas, the haku mele, the song-weavers, the word-sorters, stepped forth—and chanted the meeting of bone with bone, the flow of blood back to the heart, chanted the mele of the fathers of Paka'a, back as far as memory reached into the deep blue night of time. The son of La'amaomao had come into his own.

When the people of Hawai'i learned that Paka'a was Ku-a-Nu'uanu's own son and the new personal attendant of Keawe-nui-a-'Umi, they were glad. All over the island, the people were glad. The boy had dared to break the kapu, trusting his right that was hidden to others. He was handsome, he was generous, he was just. He would be a good kahu, like his father. A backbone held up the king to his people.

As Paka'a grew older, he learned care in courtly duties. He learned the laws of the heavens and of earth—of the stars and their highways and their meaning for men; of navigation by current, wind, and star, and the flight of birds; of steering the great double canoes of the king; of all kinds of fishing, and the cultivation of the earth. So great were his skills that the king gave him lands.

Some of these lands Paka'a shared with his former companions from Kaua'i. When Pai'ea returned to his own land, returned with honor and wealth, helped by the king and Paka'a, many of his retainers chose to remain on Hawai'i, loyal to the now powerful young chief.

And when that much smaller cloud of canoes swept back over the straits to Kaua'i, there was weeping at the welcome, for those who had returned and for those who did not return. Many canoes in that group bore provisions for La'amaomao, mother of Paka'a. Pai'ea and the chiefs who had gone made famous the honor and wealth of Paka'a, favorite of Keawe-nui-a-'Umi, a noble now of great bundles and many lands.

How was it possible for a worthless one to rise so? People simply could not believe—until, as regularly as the winds blew from the east, the canoes came with rich gifts for La'amaomao. Suddenly, people and chiefs were of one mind. The outcast became a favorite in Kapa'a. Then—the cousins and the friends sprouted on the doorstep of La'amaomao like new grass after the rains.

When Paka'a was twenty-five, his father fell ill. The kahuna came and made offerings of fine kapa and sacrifices of pigs and fowl to the gods; but in the old man's chest the breath of life fought against the strangle of death. Ku-a-Nu'uanu called Paka'a to him. Before the whole court, before Keawe-nui-a-'Umi the king, the chiefs, and the people, the dying man spoke his last words to his son. The smoke rose in a thin stream from the altar, rose high to join the great clouds scudding from east to west.

"O my son, my days are few. I leave my king in your care. Listen to his small wish, listen to his great demand. The food that is not eaten, dry it in the sun and put it in the long gourd for the time without sun. Keep it safe with the fresh fish, the live fish, the fresh 'awa, the dry 'awa. Care for what lives and for what finds it hard to live. Care for all, for high and for low. My lands are yours. I give you my master. O son of mine! O my king! Aloha!"

Like the light wind that stirs the leaves and ruffles the shallows and then dies without warning, so Ku-a-Nu'uanu passed into the spirit world.

For days there was great mourning in the land. The king and his people wept bitterly for the beloved chief who had been mindful of the weak as well as the strong.

When the days of the kapu of the dead were over, Paka'a became chief officer, and attendant to Keawe-nui-a-'Umi. As the father's place fell to the son, so did the mantle of the king's love now enfold Paka'a. He became the backbone of the king.

CHAPTER THREE

Hawai'i was at peace. Kahiku-o-ka-moku was prime
minister and the king's friend. The chiefs in charge of the
six districts of the island were all close to the king:

Makaha, ruler of Ka-'u,
Hua'a, ruler of Puna,
Kulukulu'a, ruler of Hilo,
Wanu'a, ruler of Hamakua,
Wahilani, ruler of Kohala,
And 'Ehu, ruler of Kona.

But closest of all, and the great favorite, was Paka'a.

He supervised the king's lands and directed the king's
servants. In his keeping were the king's kapas, the king's
food—the flesh food, the dry food, the fish, the poi—the
malos, the kahilis, the 'awa bowls, the cups, the 'awa itself,
the unguents, the oils—all things that gave care and comfort
to the king.

Did the mountains hide in mist? Did the winds rage?
Would the sky be black and the water white? The great
canoe of Keawe-nui-a-'Umi—would it sail that day? Would
it wait? Paka'a was the sailing master. He watched. He
steered. He was the one to decide.

So expert was Paka'a, even more so than his father,
that the king raised him over all other chiefs, over all the
people, and from each of the six districts gave him lands.
And because he was just to those of high rank and low
rank, Paka'a had the people's love as well as the king's.

41

After the fire and the sun-death,
The dark night and the climbing stars.
See there, that brightness!
It shines!
But the clouds rise and part and mass again,
And the night is black.

At the court of Keawe-nui-a-'Umi were two men, Ho'okele-i-Hilo, Steer-to-Hilo, and Ho'okele-i-Puna, Steer-to-Puna, skilled navigators both. They knew the moods of heaven and of earth, the days of good weather and bad, all the rules of their craft; but they lacked the calabash of the winds that gave Paka'a power over the winds.

These two coveted the honor of Paka'a, his power, his place. So they went before the king and boasted of their skills; they lied about Paka'a; they flattered the king. The truth of their skills masked the untruth of their words. The king's own kapu kept him from going out among his people and seeing for himself. Keawe-nui-a-'Umi believed the lies.

The sun dims. The squall descends before the mat can be spread over the young plant, the chilled shoulders. The plant breaks, the man shivers, and the rain pits the smooth sand.

From Paka'a the king took first the trust that was warmth, then the lands that were wealth, then the canoes that were command, and gave them to the two men. They were now Paka'a's enemies.

In the beginning Paka'a could not believe what was happening. But now, of all his land, only a few plots in Hilo were left. He was a treasurer who counted out but was not a trustee, a caretaker who lived at court but did not tend. When Keawe-nui-a-'Umi and his retainers went to Hilo or some other district and collected gifts from the people, the two steersmen took their share first. What was left was for Paka'a to share with the lesser chiefs and the commoners.

As the wind changes, the leaves turn their backs. Soon the people, the chiefs and commoners too, followed the king and turned their backs on Paka'a. His two enemies, Ho'okele-i-Hilo and Ho'okele-i-Puna, had won his place. Paka'a knew that now he was nothing.

The pain that gnawed within him began to tear at his heart. He saw that his master had no more use for him; so he bowed his head and prepared to go.

He took a mantle and the king's malo, scented with maile from the deep forest, the 'awa and the cup and bowl to serve it, and put them in the calabash of La'amaomao; he took his large paddle, Lapakahoe, Flash-of-the-Paddle, named for his young half-brother, and a canoe. The canoe he covered with a mat and wrapped rolls of mats all around, lest it be seen as he carried it from the canoe house to the water.

It was in the dark of the night that Paka'a left Waipi'o, left the court of his master and friend, Keawe-nui-a-'Umi, high chief of Hawai'i.

The wounded bird left lying on the path shames the hunter. By now the two steersmen who had wronged Paka'a hated the sight of him and wished to destroy him. They spied on him as he covered the canoe; they knew that he would leave. They followed him as he set off, hoping to rob him when the canoe would capsize. They splashed the waves into his canoe with their paddles, but the water ran off the mats. In his heart Paka'a called:

"O hold, my strength!
 O speed, my canoe!
 The water widens.
 O sea, rear up, bear me away!
 I must leave
 My land!"

When Paka'a's canoe left the pali of Waipi'o, the trade winds of the land, the northeast trades, the Waipi'o wind of the hollows, blew gently and steadily, and his canoe glided swiftly over the waves.

Ho'okele-i-Hilo and his companion followed for a long time; but the night was thick, they lost the other canoe. So they gave up the chase and turned back to Waipi'o, certain that Paka'a was gone, never to return.

When dawn broke, Paka'a heard the great drum of the surf off the cliffs of Hamakua, with no reef to break the might of ocean. By evening, he and his—the canoe, the calabash, and the paddle—drew near to Hilo.

The young chief Lapakahoe ruled those few lands that still belonged to Paka'a. He was amazed to see the high chief, his brother, come so, bent in sadness. After the greeting, the weeping, and the story of how it was.

"My master no longer cares for me. He has taken from me all I owned. Only these lands are left, and in time they too will go. Live on these lands. Keep faith and serve. I go I know not where. Aloha!"

Taking his calabash and his paddle, Paka'a went to his canoe on the beach, boarded it, and paddled away.

CHAPTER FOUR

Paka'a, alone on the wide sea, paddled all the night, with the east wind blowing west. He saw the small stars climb the dome of heaven and sink to their pits in the sea-rim. He thought of the boy who had come, a nothing in the train of his chief, to seek the chief his father where the Great Star of Kane rises in the east. Now the man, once more a nothing, sailed away, with the dawn-bloom behind him.

But in that vast space, with the morning winds ruffling the waters, his hurt began to heal and his heart to hope. He reached Maui, where he rested, then paddled on until he came to Moloka'i, to a place below Ho'olehua.

When the people of the place saw the lone canoe and the spent paddler, they rushed down to the beach.

"Aloha! Rest here with us!" They welcomed Paka'a as friend.

He came with little; but where is the mantle that can hide the chief? On that shore lived Hikauhi, the beautiful daughter of the high chiefs, Ho'olehua and his wife Iloli. They had promised her to one Pala'au; but once she had laid eyes on Paka'a, she could look at no one else. So Ho'olehua gave the family of Pala'au gifts, the youth stepped aside, and the girl had her way.

Paka'a and Hikauhi were married, and so began his new life. He was an expert fisherman; from childhood he had known how to cultivate the land. He and his ate well; they had sound houses.

When a little son was born to Hikauhi, Paka'a named the boy Ku, after the first part of his father's name, and Paka'a, lest the skin of his master be forgotten. Ku-a-Paka'a, named with love, to stand in the place of Paka'a. So it would be.

> The sea crashes on the coast;
> The black cloud rips
> In the sea wind!
> Then—O gladness!
> Opens up the clear sky;
> The sun!

The father forgot his grief in his joy—in the lovely mother, in the strong baby with the big hunger. He prayed to the gods:

"O Ku, Lono, Kane, and Kanaloa!
 Planted is this seed...
 Keep him safe;
 Give him long life!"

Ku was the cherished one, the favorite of his parents. Hikauhi and Paka'a brought up the baby with great care. As soon as he could walk and talk, his father began to

teach him the duties of a backbone to the king, the things a very little boy could do.

"One day my master will miss me. He will come for me. He will need your help. You are Ku-a-Paka'a. You must be ready."

Paka'a began to teach Ku all he knew. He taught him the meles he had chanted for Keawe-nui-a-'Umi. He taught him the names of all the winds and the chants to call them, just as his mother La'amaomao had taught him many years ago. The boy learned them all.

In the late afternoon Ku and his friends would seek out a little tidal pool in the rocks by the sea. One boy would act as judge. Then, two at a time, the others would lie down with their chests to the lava, gazing into the pool, facing the setting sun. Who could last the longest?
Each took a deep breath, then whispered slowly to himself:

"Na'u-u-u-u-u-u-u-u-u-u-u-u-u-..."

"For me-me-me-me-me-me-me-me-...the rays of the sun!" The sun set; the sky turned orange, then blood-red, then violet. Group by group, the children would na'u until dark.

The sea was nurse and school and teacher. Who could race farthest on the hard sand by the water's edge—without taking a breath? Who could stay under water longest? Ku-a-Paka'a.

The boy would stand alone on the beach until his face grew red and his eyes started, chanting the waves, echoing the breakers that gathered power, that broke and fell, over and over, the endless waves.

49

When his father went to the forest, Ku would go with
him and chant the gurgle of the small stream, the calm flow
of the big stream, the deep roar of the waterfall. In time,
he had the strong lungs of one who chants for a king. His
tones made music. Ku-a-Paka'a was ready.

50

Meanwhile, all was not well at Waipi'o. As long as Paka'a was at the court of Keawe-nui-a-'Umi, his two enemies served the king well. What they did not know, Paka'a knew. What they did not do, Paka'a did. The backbone held up his king and the king's kahili.

But now Paka'a had gone.

At first, Keawe-nui-a-'Umi hardly felt his loss, so charmed was he with his new favorites. The two still told tales about Paka'a; the king still believed them.

On the waters, on the great canoe, the two were master steersmen; but once sure of their place at court, they began to swagger, to neglect the king. They were careless of his person, of his malos. From the gifts that were sent him, they chose the best and gave him their leavings. He questioned them, and they lied. He called, and they did not answer.

At the heiau, at the feast, at the sacred ceremony, the priests chanted the line of the king, back through his father Great 'Umi and his mother Kapukini, back through the sky life, back through the earth life, back through the sea life, back to the Bright One, the Sky God. The king to be loved, the king to be feared, the king to be served; the king, a god among men.

But the king, Keawe-nui-a-'Umi, was lonely and miserable. He missed his friend whom he had wronged. Full of scorn for his two helmsmen, full of shame for himself, the king wailed and wept hot tears.

51

Where now was the bone that did not bend, the heart that wore no mask, the care that did not tire? Where? O where was Paka'a? Auwe!

Keawe-nui-a-'Umi sent for the seers, the kahunas, and soothsayers. What to do? Where to turn?

The wise men studied the clouds, the stars in the heavens, all the omens of earth and sky. They were of one mind.

"Paka'a lives; but where he lives—that is hidden from us. Wait before you seek him. Give word to the chiefs and commoners to go up to the uplands to build canoes. Many canoes must be built before the king can look to find the one he loves."

So the canoe-makers hurried to the high, wet forests to cut the koa logs. Those who could not go stayed in the valley to till the soil and prepare food for the others.

The task would not be easy.

Rains marched upon the forest and lashed trees and men.

"I have found a tree, a fine large tree!" Again and again the cry rang out; but as soon as the adzes of the canoe-makers struck the wood of the tree, two woodpeckers pecked and chirped on that tree. "This tree is hollow!"

So it happened with tree after tree. When each tree chosen stood to topple, the same two 'elepaio cried their cry.

"The birds are crying! This tree is hollow!"

Archers loosed their arrows, slingers flung their stones, snarers cast their nets and spread their gum—but who could kill the birds?

Who indeed? For the birds were personal gods of Paka'a come to test the aloha of the king for his friend. Could he hold fast in his aim to find Paka'a?

There was one archer who never missed, Pikoi-a-ka-'alala, the Bold, a hunter of rats and of birds in flight. The fame of his arrows was known from Kaua'i to Hawai'i. Keawe-nui-a-'Umi sent his messenger to fetch the man.

Pikoi guessed the mission.

"Is that you?" he said to the messenger.

"'Ae."

"Your purpose?"

"I am sent by Keawe-nui-a-'Umi to fetch you to come and shoot the birds that trouble him where he makes

53

canoes in the uplands. Each tree cut the birds prove hollow."

"Let us go. Your king has a burden. Those must be birds with miraculous powers."

They hurried to the uplands, to the king, where he waited.

The next morning again the cry rang out, "I have found a tree!" This time Pikoi-a-ka-'alala went with the king and the kahunas who carved.

"Listen now to the ax!
This is the ax that will fell the tree!"

As soon as the ax cut into the tree flesh, a bird soared overhead and hovered to alight on a branch. Pikoi loosed his arrow that did not miss, and the bird fluttered and tumbled to the ground. The second bird startled in its flight to see its mate so falter. Pikoi sped his second arrow and downed the second bird. But when people looked for the small bodies at the base of the tree, they were nowhere. No one saw the birds again.

Now the work leaped.

"Smite with the ax and hollow the canoe!
Grant us a canoe swift as a fish!"

In a short time the king and his men returned to the valley dragging many rough canoes to be fashioned in the canoe house. The king held fast to his aim.

CHAPTER SIX

One day a canoe pulled in to Moloka'i from Hilo.

"I bring news from Hawai'i."

"What is your news?"

"Keawe-nui-a-'Umi is building canoes. He will go in search of his man Paka'a."

The news startled Paka'a, but he did not make himself known to the man from Hilo. Instead, he went to his hut and lay down to relax and think what he should do. Could friendship, like an old net laid aside, be mended and used once more? Stretched out so, with his legs crossed and his feet against the wall of the hut, he fell asleep, and dreamed a dream; his spirit met the spirit of Keawe-nui-a-'Umi.

"I am looking for you."

"If you are looking for me, I am on Ka'ula."

Paka'a sat up with a start. The dream had been like life. Aloha for his master rushed up in his heart, and rue that he had led him astray. For Ka'ula was an islet far off to the west, near Kaua'i, a home of birds.

Then he thought, should Keawe-nui-a'Umi come in search of Paka'a and land on Moloka'i, he would plan for the king to stay awhile, but he, Paka'a, would not make himself known. He would set his son Ku-a-Paka'a to care for the king, to be his personal attendant. The king would mark the skill of the boy and no doubt ask him to return with him to Hawai'i. That would be the end of Ho'okele-i-Hilo and Ho'okele-i-Puna. When his enemies were destroyed, when the backbone would be free once more to

stand as pillar, then Paka'a would return to Hawai'i. Then
Keawe-nui-a-'Umi would find Paka'a.

But a small house could not hold the king and the
chiefs of Hawai'i who would come with him. The next
morning Paka'a called to his son.

"Let's go up to the hills for wood and grass. Your
master and his chiefs are coming to look for me. They will
need houses. You must be ready."

" 'Ae. Let's go."

At last Ku would see his master with the stronghold in
his father's heart. The boy ran ahead of his father up the
hillside to seek out the straight trees, the tall trees for the
long rafters, the short trees for the short posts. Plant the
posts deep in earth, lash them firm, bind on the pili thatch,
a sweet smell for the house, a mantle for the hot sun, for
the cold rain, for the harsh wind.

56

Six chiefs would come. Paka'a and his son built six houses.

"Let's go and plant food. Feed your king well, and you will keep him content."

" 'Ae. Let's go."

Six fields of cane, six strips of potato patch Paka'a and his son planted, one of each for the six districts of Hawai'i.

"Let's go to the hills again for leaves of the fan palm."

" 'Ae. Let's go."

They brought down enough leaves to fill a whole hut.

"This is enough. Now we are ready," said Paka'a. "Now we can wait."

It was at this moment that the two birds, the gods of Paka'a that had troubled the canoe-builders of Keawe-nui-a-'Umi, knew their work was finished, and let themselves fall to the arrows of Pikoi.

The news of the search for Paka'a spread far and wide over all the islands of Hawai'i. People asked, "Where is this Paka'a?" No one could say.

One night Keawe-nui-a-'Umi dreamed a dream; his spirit met the spirit of Paka'a.

"I am looking for you."

"If you are looking for me, I am on Ka'ula."

Keawe-nui-a-'Umi awoke with his mind at ease. In the morning he sent for his kahunas, those who read the stars, and the two steersmen. He told them his dream.

The wise men pondered. "The gods hide the place of Paka'a. There is no Paka'a on Ka'ula."

"The canoes are ready. When should we sail?"

"You should sail in the days of Ku," the priests agreed.

That night again the king dreamed, and again he met the spirit of Paka'a.

"I am ready to go in search of you."

Again came the reply, "If you are looking for me, I am on Ka'ula."

"In the days of Ku we will search for you."

Keawe-nui-a-'Umi started and awoke. The dream upset him. The priests had said there was no Paka'a on Ka'ula. But he and his chiefs would set out, they would sail from island to island, across the wide waters, even to the far west. Keawe-nui-a-'Umi would not rest until he had found Paka'a.

CHAPTER SEVEN

Came the days of Ku and the canoes of Keawe-nui-a-'Umi were ready to sail from Waipi'o. In the dawn they gathered, dappling the waters like a flock of kolea, eager for the quest, for the long flight. First the ten canoes with a single man, then the ten with two men, then ten with three, until there were many men in each canoe; then the double canoes with supplies, then the canoe with the second in command, the canoes with the women, the canoes with soldiers. Then began the double canoes of the chiefs:

> Wahilani, chief of Kohala,
> Wanu'a, chief of Hamakua,
> Kulukulu'a, chief of Hilo,
> Hua'a, chief of Puna,
> Makaha, chief of Ka-'u,
> And 'Ehu, chief of Kona.

And last of all came Keawe-nui-a-'Umi and his prime minister, Kahiku-o-ka-moku, on the great double canoe with the platform in the middle.

Let all men see that fleet and know what love Keawe-nui-a-'Umi bore Paka'a.

The canoes sailed, like sea birds, seeking. They landed on Maui, at Lahaina. The call of the conch trumpet on the lead canoe brought the people crowding to the shore.

"Have you seen the man Paka'a?"

"We have not seen him."

That was the first of the four days of Ku. After a night, the fleet sailed on.

In the very early dawn of the second of the days of Ku, the fourth day of the month, Paka'a wakened his son Ku-a-Paka'a.

"Say, you who are asleep, we should get up lest your master pass by and we miss him."

By starlight the two got out the gear, the lines and hooks to fish for uhu, the wind calabash of La'amaomao, went to the beach, boarded their small canoe, and set off.

Paka'a took the bow seat, holding the fishline, bending his head as if to fish uhu, lest he be seen by his king.

By the inboard lashing of the outrigger boom Ku placed the wind calabash of La'amaomao. Then, taking up his father's big paddle, Lapakahoe, the boy took the stern

seat, to paddle, to steer. No sooner did they drop their
stone anchor at the fishing ground than the first canoes of
Keawe-nui-a-'Umi began to arrive. When the double canoes
of the chiefs drew near, a torch blazed over the waters near
Kaunakakai.

"Say there! That's a big fire! It must be my master!"

"That's not he," said Paka'a.

"Then who is it?"

"That's Wahilani, ruling over Kohala."

"Is he a king?"

"Not a king."

The fine double canoe of Wahilani glided by. Ku-a-
Paka'a called out in a loud voice:

"Wahilani sailed by, our chief of Kohala.
  He's no chief by birth, but a petty chief only,
  Who hides in a cane clump.
  The flesh-food of that land, the locust,
  That feeds on the cane leaf, the grass flower.
  A land without fish, sweet potatoes its food,
  That's the food of Kohala;
  That's what's wrong with the land.
  And they say, 'Call him chief!'"

One of Wahilani's men asked, "Who is it calls to our chief?"

"I wonder who," said Ku. "It is night. No one can see."

Wahilani was angry. "Where did you learn all this, false boy? Paddle on!"

The canoe of Wahilani lunged off, but a torch still blazed.

"Say! There's another fire! Perhaps it's my master's canoe."

"Not that."

"Who is it?"

"That's Wanu'a, owner of Hamakua."

"Is he a king?"

"Not a king."

Wanu'a's canoe went sailing by them. Ku-a-Paka'a called out:

"Here comes that person called Wanu'a,
  That chief of ours from Hamakua.

He's no chief, but a petty chief,
A snarer of eels from Hamakua.
He spreads his fingers on the rock,
Snares the small eels, after bait.
He chucks them in his calabash,
Food for one meal.
Now he's ruler of Hamakua.
They call him 'Chief,' but he's no chief!"

"Who is that person who calls to our chief?"

"I wonder who," said Ku. "Who can see in the dark?"

Wanu'a frowned. His canoe spurted off. Another torch glared on the water.

"Could that be my chief coming up now?"

"That's not your chief; that's Kulukulu'a, who rules over Hilo."

"Is he a chief?"

"He's no chief," said Paka'a.

Kulukulu'a's canoe swept near, and Ku-a-Paka'a called out:

"There goes Kulukulu'a, our chief from Hilo,
No chief he, but a petty chief,
A snarer of shrimps from Waiakea.
Once he snares them,
He wears the snare on his ear.
Now he rules over Hilo;
They call him a chief!"

"Who speaks there so loudly to our chief?"

"No one knows. No one can see. It is too dark." Ku smiled to himself.

The angry Kulukulu'a had hardly passed by when another torch flared up.

"Maybe the next one is my chief."

"That's not your chief; that's Hua'a, ruler of Puna."

"Is he a high chief?"

"No high chief," said Paka'a.

They finished talking, and Hua'a's canoe went sailing by. Ku-a-Paka'a called:

> "Hua'a sailed by, our chief from Puna,
>   No high chief he, but a petty chief,
>   Thorny eyes of the hala from Puna.
>   They call him a chief,
>   But he's no chief!"

"Who in the world calls so to our chief?"

"Who knows?" said Ku. "We can't see him in the dark."

Hua'a sped off in a huff. Another flare glittered over the water.

"Is the next one my master?"

"Not he. That's Makaha, who has Ka-'u."

"Is he a chief?"

"Not a chief," said Paka'a.

Makaha's canoe drew near, and Ku-a-Paka'a called:

"There goes our chief of Ka-'u, called Makaha.
He's no high chief, just a petty chief.
Dirty eyes of Ka-'u, 'ilima leaf-washer of Kama'oa
Washes the leaves in dirty bath water.
Clean body and dirty ears,
He's ruler of Ka-'u;
They call him a high chief!"

Makaha rushed off in a fury, his men plunging their paddles deep in the foam. One more torch glowed in the gray dawn light.
"Maybe this next one is my chief."
"That's not your chief, that's 'Ehu, over Kona."
"Is he a high chief?"
"He's no chief; he's a potato grower from Napu'u."
'Ehu's canoe sailed past, and Ku-a-Paka'a called out:

" 'Ehu sailed by, our chief from Kona.
He's no high chief;
He's a potato pusher from Napu'u.
With Keawe-nui-a-'Umi we lived at Kiholo;
'Ehu came down from the uplands with bags
    of potatoes.
The king ate so long and so well on that land,
He called 'Ehu son,
He gave 'Ehu Kona.
Now they call 'Ehu chief!"

"Who is the man who speaks so to our chief?"

"Who knows?" said Ku. "We can't see in this light."

To each chief Ku called out what he had learned about them from his father. But the night was fast turning to day. The rising clouds scudded before the dawn wind and the east bloomed with light.

Ku-a-Paka'a asked Paka'a, "Oh, when will my master come?"

"When you see the rays of the sun, then you will see your master. His sail is notched to let all know it is he. His god is Ka'ili, standing before. His seat is on the high place, with the helmsmen behind. He will arrive out of the arch of the dawn."

While they spoke the sun rose. Ku saw the great canoe approach in a blaze of light, its sides glittering, the paddles of the men blinding in their flash. He looked to the high place in the middle and saw the face of his king carved against the morning.

CHAPTER EIGHT

"Here comes my chief!"

" 'Ae. That is your master! That is your king! That is his canoe!"

"Ku'u haku! Ku'u ali'i!"

The splendor of the awaited one dazzled the boy. Near the prow he could see the red-feathered god of 'Umi and Liloa, wrapped in pure white kapa. On the pola he could see Keawe-nui-a-'Umi in his crested helmet and mantle of feathers. He could see the proud chiefs around him.

The six canoes of the chiefs of Hawai'i had moved off to a distance. The great canoe of Keawe-nui-a-'Umi and the small canoe of Paka'a were alone on the water.

"Where is he now?" Paka'a kept his head bent over the fishline.

"On our outside, toward the sea."

"Hold up your paddle."

Keawe-nui-a-'Umi would know the sign that his backbone had heeded when he was helmsman.

Ku-a-Paka'a held upright the big steering paddle, Lapakahoe, to show that he would speak. Among the king's retainers on the great canoe was Lapakahoe himself, the younger half-brother of Paka'a, come from Hilo to help seek his brother. When he spied the paddle he called out to the king.

"Say! There's a small canoe floating on our shore side. Someone holds up a paddle. Let's sail toward it!"

The two helmsmen grumbled, "Why should we sail there just because that boy holds up his paddle?"

Keawe-nui-a-'Umi spoke up from his high seat under the awning, "O you two who are now my helmsmen, do you wonder that I seek Paka'a? Paka'a heeds the man of high rank and the man of no rank, the great fleet and the lone canoe, like that small canoe that floats there by itself. He hearkens to the man who invites him and to the one who holds up his paddle. Perhaps that one has a word for us, perhaps he has fish and poi. We sail on the wide ocean, who knows for how long? You two head the bow of the canoe toward that small one."

The helmsmen set the bow of the great canoe toward shore. Paka'a waited a bit; then he asked Ku, "Where now is your lord?"

"Here he is, quite close."

"Then call out what your lord is to do."

Ku called out loud and clear across the water:

> "Hold back there! Hold back!
> Be still there! Be still!
> Be calm there! Be calm!
> Gently there! Gently!
> Listen to the call,
> The query, the question!
> The call of this child:
> Whose the canoe?"

The men on the great canoe called back, "This is the canoe of Keawe-nui-a-'Umi."

"A canoe sailing where?"

"A canoe sailing to seek Paka'a."

"Look for Paka'a and find him! Who is Paka'a?"

"He is a servant."

Ku muttered to his father, "I thought you were a chief, and here you are a servant."

Paka'a whispered to the boy to ask again.

"Is he really a servant?" Ku called.

"Not really a servant, but bearer of the king's kahili, keeper of the king's anointing oils, carer of the king's person, of his hair—his backbone."

Ku was relieved. He whispered to his father, "Then you are a chief, if you touch the king's head! With your rank as chief and my mother's rank as chiefess, I shall be quite a chief here on Moloka'i."

Paka'a smiled. "Then hold the head high and chant the name of your chief and your greeting."

So Ku chanted the chant that he had learned from his father:

> "So the canoes are yours,
>   O the great Hawai'i of Kane,
>   O great Hawai'i, land of the sun,
>   Of the sun that rises, the high-riding sun,
>   Keawe-nui-a-'Umi who sits there,
>   The canoes are yours."

Kahiku-o-ka-moku, the prime minister of the king, answered with a chant:

"Then you, child, do not know,
    You do not know the canoes
    Belong to Ku, belong to Lono,
    Belong to Kane and Kanaloa,
    Belong to the myriad spirits,
    To the legion of gods.
    This is a canoe from the rainy land
    Of Hilo of Malama,
    The canoes belong to Keawe-nui-a-'Umi."

Ku called back:

"So yours are the canoes,
    O Hilo rain that overwhelms rain..."

And the memories that flooded the heart of the father
burst forth in the voice of the child:

"So that is your canoe...
The birthplace of the storm is here.
Clean-swept and dark is the crest of Mount Aluli,
Like a black kapa, the cloud
Blows across the face of Kawaikapu cliff,
Torn by the wind that runs in the hollows,
That holds back the waters...
O the voice of the Kuaiwa grindstone,
The voice of the weeping grindstone
Whetting the churning sea.
Swing the burden to the back,
Hug the child to the breast,
Slack the bow line.
The lordly clouds of Wailau gather,
Gather and mass at the brow of the cliff,
Pueo-hulu-nui, where the owls fly.
And so the canoe is yours."

When the boy had finished, Kahiku-o-ka-moku asked him, "Young one, how did you learn these chants?"

"Oh, the children of this place learn chants with their first poi."

"We are going to sail. If you have a word for us, speak it."

"I called to urge you people to go ashore. There's fish and there's poi. Sail tomorrow, the calm day. This is a stormy day. The clouds are massing above Kainui. While the weather is bad, stay."

Overhead the bowl of heaven was a clear blue. "We see no signs of a storm." The helmsmen scoffed at Ku. "If the king's canoes land at this rough place, they will smash to pieces. Will your bones be the pegs to fill the holes, to put them together again?"

Ku whispered to his father, "Could that be?"

Paka'a told Ku what to answer.

"Say! Men's bones don't peg a canoe. The adz fells the tree and lops off the branches. The adz carves the outside and hollows out the inside. Pig and dog bones, not men's bones, bore the holes for the lashings, give polish to the canoe."

The other men on the great canoe cheered Ku. "You are right, boy. When the water in the spring dries up, the mud rises. Those two spoke rudely."

"But I have a question," spoke Kahiku-o-ka-moku. "How can this day be stormy? We can see the tops of the mountains, the shapes in the cloud banks."

"This is a stormy, a windy day. You people come from Hawai'i, a windy place, and there it blows behind you!"

Ku-a-Paka'a knew his land well. Calm it might be in the morning, but at noon, the trade winds would come up and blow ever more strongly.

"How do you know about the winds of Hawai'i? Perhaps you have not seen the place?"

"Over here on Moloka'i such chants are the playthings of children. I can chant you the winds of Hawai'i, winds that will be the death of you all!"

"Let's hear them!"

So Ku-a-Paka'a chanted the winds of Hawai'i that his father had taught him, to ready him for this moment—the winds of Hilo, of Puna, the trade that bows tall men short, the Kona wind that tosses up the sea spray.

CHAPTER NINE

The men on the king's canoe called out, "Are you through with the winds of Hawai'i?"

"Not through. There are more. But there's no use tiring my mouth for nothing. If you people agree to land, I'll go on. No helmsman could steer you to O'ahu today."

Kahiku-o-ka-moku turned to the kahunas. "Is this really a stormy day?"

The wise men scanned the heavens. "No storm will come this clear day."

The helmsmen demanded that they leave the boy and his talk and sail. But the quick wits of Ku amused the king and his chiefs. One of them braced his paddle. They wanted to hear more. So the great canoe drifted.

75

"There they are! There they are!
The winds of the land..."

Ku called on the winds of Hawai'i. One by one, he
named them all, from the sudden-shower wind of Waimea
to the flying-whale wind of Hamakua. Then his chant darkened to a warning:

"The tail of that wind,
The tail of this wind,
Twist into a whirlwind.
The death canoe will have freight to hold.
Death swamps the small canoe,
It will swamp the large canoe.
At dawn the chief dies, the priest dies,
The weak one dies, the strong one dies,
The dark strong one, the light strong one,
The seeker, the seer,
Scanning the sign in the breakers,
The red star, the lei of stars.
Would that your canoe had come
Yesterday when it was calm.
Say there, Keawe-nui-a-'Umi, land!
It is stormy!"

"Say!" Kahiku-o-ka-moku called out. "The chief's
canoes will not land just because you ask it, boy. Those
winds you chanted are of Hawai'i. No Hawai'i wind can
reach Moloka'i."

"Well, there's another windy land ahead, O'ahu.

"There's the cloud of me and my father;
The cause of the storm is what the child warns."

Ku chanted the blustery wind of Waiala'e, the hide-and-
seek wind of Kalihi, the house-beating wind of Honolulu;
he chanted the raging-sea wind of Waianae, the bird-gather-
ing wind of Kahuku, the blow-along-the-cliff wind of Kualoa
and Ka'a'awa, the whirlwind of the Nu'uanu uplands, the
gentle breeze of Kailua.

> "When it blows from before,
> You will all be caught,
> You will be caught, O unheeding chief...
> You will be caught by the fisherman
> In a net with a small hole...
> You'll be bait, you'll be sliced up,
> And that wrinkled thing will be eaten
> By insects and crabs...
> Listen to my life-saving warning,
> O Keawe-nui-a-'Umi, lord, land!
> It is stormy!"

The men on the great canoe now stood puzzled. They
half believed the boy. They feared their death. The two
canoes, the great and the small, drifted there in the morning
light.

Then Lapakahoe called, "You are smart, young fellow, and we like to hear the chants and winds of Hawai'i and O'ahu. But are those the only windy lands?"

"Kaua'i is a windy land.

"Arise. Look you to the winds of La'amaomao,
   Roaring in the mountains..."

Ku chanted the winds of Kaua'i, from the wind-cloud cliff of Kapa'a to the Limahuli of Ha'ena, where men held their canoe paddles against the dripping cliffs to catch the fresh water.

But hardly had Ku finished when the men drifting there heard a great roar.

"You have angered the winds," Paka'a told the boy. "First you called the winds of Hawai'i to the far east; then you should have called the wind of Ka'ula to the far west."

So Ku chanted the wind of Ka'ula:

"Down by the rock of Ola,
   The black bird begged,
   The bird of Ka'ula begged...
   Floating up there above Wa'ahila...
   The soaring-wing wind is the wind of Ka'ula;
   Give me, give me, give me the wind!"

Keawe-nui-a-'Umi now spoke. "Boy, you are quite a wit. I have told you that I sail the ocean in search of Paka'a, and here you call out, 'Give me the wind!' I will not land on your shore!" And the king called out to his helmsmen, Ho'okele-i-Hilo and Ho'okele-i-Puna, "Let's sail!"

But the boy had whetted the curiosity of Lapakahoe. When the men in the rear of the canoe dipped their paddles to get under way, he bade the men forward to stall and brace theirs. So they dug their paddles deep, the pebbles on the bottom growled, and sand eddied up around the great canoe, held fast as if by an anchor.

By now the king was angry. Ku whispered to his father, "A storm rises in my master's heart. He wills to go!"

"Then chant *his* storm," said Paka'a.

"Hurry! Hurry! Hurry!
Hasten that way, hasten this way,
The ocean is a lei around your neck.
Go you are tricked, stay you are tricked;
The green-black hawk is in the sky,
It is a windy day.
The rain falls, the rivers gush,
The shrimps come up, the sea-caves are bared.
Where the sea foams, the moi dwell;
Where the sea tosses, the mullet spawn.
When the tide ebbs, spear the squid,
Scrape up the sea-eggs, hook the large sea-eggs.
The turtles come up to breathe on a windy day.
Where the sea is murky, live the manini;
Where the shoals are rocky, the uoa turns;
Where the sea is deep blue, there dwell the sharks;
At the deep fishing ground, troll the kahala.
Spit out the kukui nut, the sea becomes calm,
Pull in the uhu;
Then go ahead, go silently, go noisily.

The pointed clouds are in the heavens,
The heart of the rain is in the heavens.
The streams swell,
The thunder pounds, the earth quakes,
The lightning blazes in the sky.

The small rain, the big rain,
The long rain, the short rain,
The rain of wintry sleep,
Stops the breath, flattens the hair,
Parts the hair in the middle.
Sleep curled up, sleep face up,
Sleep and listen; sleep, then awaken.
The teeth gnash in anger, but the arm lags;
The stubborn chief dies.
Calm him, hold him, you headstrong helmsmen,
The ocean will kill you all...
Take care of the favorite child
Lest he be lost in the sea of Kaulua.
Let the canoe land!
There's food ashore, there's kapa, there's malo.
Live out the stormy days;
When it is calm, then go,
Then sail away, my master."

The king heard the boy's aloha for his master in his chant; his anger cooled.

But Lapakahoe leaned forward over one of the bow pieces of the great canoe and listened ever more intently. Aloha for his missing brother rushed up in his heart. The boy was chanting as he and Paka'a had chanted together. Who could have taught the boy?

"Boy, who taught you what you know?"

"But I have already told you, children here on Moloka'i pick up these chants very easily."

"Then it is Paka'a who has taught you. Listen, boy, is Paka'a on land at this place?"

"Paka'a is not on this land," Ku answered, "but we have heard of such a man living on Ka'ula."

It was as in the king's dream. Lapakahoe fell silent and asked no more.

All this time the fisherman bent over his line at the front of the small canoe. Kahiku-o-ka-moku called out to Ku, "Who is that at the bow of your canoe?"

"Oh, that is just my father. He is deaf. He likes to troll uhu." And to draw their minds off his father Ku took up his chant and his warning:

> "Hurry! Hurry! Hurry!
> The wave welcomes the castaway.
> Here am I, O death!
> Death to you is the small wave,
> Death to you is the large wave,
> Death to you is the long wave,

Death to you is the short wave,
The wave of death will swamp your canoe.
The bow-piece breaks, the stern-pieces fly,
The priest is wrenched from the king;
Their bond breaks on the day of death.
Your honor, O helmsmen, O priests, is at stake!
Know the star of the land there, and land!"

Fear chilled the heart of Keawe-nui-a-'Umi. Again he asked the wise men, "Shall we go ashore?"

And again they answered, "Where are the storm clouds, where the winds, that we should believe this boy? Today's children are false. This is the day you sail to Ka'ula and find Paka'a."

Ku heard them. He whispered to Paka'a, "E ku'u makuakane, they say I lie. They will not land."

"Then chant the open-mouth warning."

"The sea snares the eyes
And hides the line of islands.
Death you will meet in the days of Ku,
Days when the foam sucks outward,
The current flows seaward.
The shark's mouth will open,
The wave's mouth will open,
Will gulp you down and you die,
    O Keawe-nui-a-'Umi.
You will go back to Hawai'i a spirit.
Come ashore, it is stormy!"

83

The helmsmen called back:

"Who would land on such a fine day?
  Where, boy, is the storm you speak of today?"

"Oh, but listen," said Ku.

"There's the fish of me and my father,
  A hinalea gone back to its cave,
  Curled up there, curled up here because
      of the storm.
  There's the uhu of me and my father,
  Coming here to the edge of the net,
  Showing its teeth in rage at the storm.
  There's the coconut of me and my father,
  Planted in the ocean, grew in the ocean,
  Bore fruit in the ocean, grew ripe in the ocean.
  The coconut squeaks, it squeaks in the storm."

"Boy, you lie. Where is the storm? Where is the coconut that grows in the ocean?"
  "Can't the ears that stand on your head hear?"
  Kahiku-o-ka-moku called, "We hear the squeak of the
sennit lashings of our canoe."
  "Then don't coconuts grow in the ocean?"
  "Boy, you annoy us! We have had enough of you and
your riddles." The helmsmen threatened Ku. "If we find
you here when we come back from O'ahu, we'll roast you
in the imu!"

Ku whispered to his father, "Could that be?" Paka'a told him what to answer.

"Not the imu but the voice it is that will kill me! You two will die in the ocean in the plain sight of all!"

The helmsmen gave the signal, the men raised their paddles, they made ready to sail.

"My master is about to sail."

"Now is the time to call the winds of Maui and Moloka'i."

So Ku called the bait-eating wind of Hana, the gnashing winds of Kula that strew snow on the uplands, the small-fish wind of Wailuku, the orange-fragrant wind of

Liloa, the dark-water wind of Hololua. He called the winds of Halawa, the wild eastern cape of his island, and the other winds of Moloka'i.

"The strong-rain wind,
  The strong tale-bearing wind,
  That forces a breach in the land at Halawa,
  The frosty night wind, the cliff-adz wind,
  The cold, the sea-spray wind of Halawa...

"The wind at Kaunakakai blows strong and cold,
  Kupeke's wind is an ear-tugging wind,
  The love-making wind is of Makaluhau,
  The wind of Nihoa is the eye of the night god...

"The harbor is there; land!
  Land while you are near, my lord;
  Land while I am near, your servant.
  Wait for the calm day.
  Look for Paka'a; find Paka'a."

When Lapakahoe heard Ku's last words, he called, "Boy, your chant was indeed good, but your words are false. Just a while ago you said Paka'a was not ashore; yet you ask us to land." Anger welled up in Lapakahoe, and he called on the paddlers to sail.

Ku-a-Paka'a had almost lost heart. He muttered, half to himself and half to his father, "There sails away that master of mine. What more can I do to hold him?"

"Chant the names of the paddlers and of your master. Perhaps they will agree to land when they hear their names."

Before the chief's paddlers could dip their paddles in the water, Ku called out the names of all the men in one and then of all those in the other of the two hulls that made up the double canoe of Keawe-nui-a-'Umi, just as his father whispered them to him.

When he finished, Kahiku-o-ka-moku called back, "You know our names, but we do not know yours. What is your name?"

"Land now at my place and I'll tell you my name."

The men had had enough. They took up their paddles, dipped them in the ocean, and the great canoe of the chief moved off. Ku watched the great canoe sail away, with the paddles flashing, the kapa streaming, the crab-claw sail turned to the wind, a proud thing! But of all the men in the canoe, only the king himself turned back to look at the boy Ku, upright in the small canoe. The water widened between them, and soon the great canoe was far enough off for Paka'a to raise his head.

CHAPTER TEN

Ku watched the glittering canoe grow smaller and smaller, until the waves hid the hulls, hid the paddlers. After the chanting and the calls, there was now only the gurgle of the waves against the sides of the small canoe.

"He will never come now. I have tired my mouth for nothing." Ku sat back and looked at his father, waiting.

Paka'a turned to look at the proud boy and thought of the boy so many years before who must wait as a slave and take the leavings of others until he would be known as son of a chief. He thought of the words of his mother: "If people taunt you, lift the lid slightly and call. The clean wind will clear the air and bear you and your canoes to land. Your chief will honor you. The calabash is yours. Use it only when you need it."

"He who serves learns patience, Ku-a-Paka'a. To listen is often to live, and to pay no heed is to die. Your master will return to you or die for having been deaf to your warnings."

By now the great canoe was almost out of sight. They could see only the sail.

Paka'a looked very intently at Ku. "Open slightly the wind calabash of La'amaomao."

Ku-a-Paka'a lifted the lid of the calabash and called:

"O winds that I have called
From Ka'ula and Kaua'i,
Blow from before;
O winds from O'ahu and Hawai'i,
Blow from the sides;
O winds of Maui and Moloka'i,
Blow from behind;
Blow!
Until you reach the fleet of Keawe-nui-a-'Umi!"

And as he called Ku felt in himself the mana of that distant grandmother.

Pointed clouds began to rise on the horizon; the bright day darkened. The black-piled storm clouds massed, while lightning blazed over the dark waters. The fountains of ocean opened and rose to meet the torrents of heaven, and the voice of the storm spoke.

When Keawe-nui-a-'Umi saw the storm signs, bitterness and fear fought within him. He upbraided the priests, the seers, the helmsmen, for not heeding Ku's warnings.

89

"It is here, the storm none of you would see. The boy said to come ashore. I asked you who should know, and all I heard was, 'This is a clear day. Where is the storm? Where are the signs?' Now the fire flashes, the thunder roars, and the god Ku makes the heavy rain fall. The winds will rip us from our canoe! This canoe is the death canoe. All the canoes may be death canoes, and we the freight for the spirit world! Auwe! Would I had gone ashore!"

The ax of the storm cleaved the fleet of Keawe-nui-a-'Umi. Swamped were the lead canoes with the chiefs and commoners. The waves towered and rolled over the swimming men, swept them into the death-dealing, the outgoing current into the great ocean.

Pushed by the winds from above, from the sides, from behind, the waves tossed, now that way, now this. When the large canoes went to the rescue of the small ones, they too were swamped. The water was strewn with bundles of kapa, with masts, with paddles, with sails. Who could say which were calabashes of poi, which were coconuts, which the wet heads of men? The storm opened its jaws to all.

The flesh on the bones was numb as death in the battering cold of the waves. Keawe-nui-a-'Umi wailed for the loss of his men and canoes, wailed for the helplessness of kings. "Now you know why I seek Paka'a! My body would never be wet, were I with Paka'a! Now we are swamped in the ocean and may die. It is just as the boy said!"

The strong swimmers tried to grab at the paddles, tried to right the canoes, but the waves rolled over them.

From the fishing ground, Paka'a and Ku watched the storm in the distance. When they saw the sail of the king waver, like a bird's wing broken, Paka'a said to Ku, "Close the calabash. Your master must be numb with cold. He could die."

So Ku-a-Paka'a closed the calabash of the winds. The clouds melted, the sea smoothed, the air warmed. The storm was over.

The people blinked to see the sun so soon. The storm went as quickly as it had come. They found their paddles, their bailing cups, righted their canoes, and climbed into them.

Keawe-nui-a-'Umi climbed up to his seat. From there he could see that Moloka'i was the nearest land. He called to the rest of the fleet gathered around the great canoe, awaiting the will of the king.

"Let's go back to Moloka'i. If the boy asks us to land, this time we shall say, 'Yes!' "

The storm had worn out the paddlers. They had lost their food, their supplies, their strength. They quickly agreed to turn back. Each was eager to get to the harbor they had once spurned before the sun would set.

The canoe of the king had more paddlers than the others and moved faster. Ku saw it arrive first. He cried out to his father, once more bent over his fishline.

"Here comes that lord of mine!"

"If he agrees to land, tell him this is a crooked channel, that we will go ahead, that they may follow when we call out to them. They must not land before we do. They must not see who I am."

When the great canoe of Keawe-nui-a-'Umi, battered and bruised, was very near, Ku called, "O my king, you have looked death in the face. Now will you land?"

"I will land," said Keawe-nui-a-'Umi.

CHAPTER ELEVEN

"My chief, this channel is crooked. My father and I will go ahead and wave you on when it is safe. Had you landed before, we would have had no trouble; the tide was low, the reef in plain sight. Now it is late, the tide is high. You might miss the course."

"You are right. Lead and we shall follow."

Ku pulled up the stone anchor, and he and his father paddled in over the reef. After a bit, Ku waved and called to the others to come on; then the two paddled on ahead. And so the two canoes zigzagged in. When they neared the shore, Ku paddled furiously, the small canoe nosed onto the beach, and Paka'a leaped onto the sand and ran up to the cookhouse, where a king and his chiefs would not go.

From his place at the bow of the great double canoe Lapakahoe saw him run. The man ran like Paka'a. But could that be...? No. Paka'a was on Ka'ula.

By evening all the canoes had landed in the calm harbor, but Keawe-nui-a-'Umi still sat on the pola of the great canoe, silent and miserable. He had not come ashore with the others because his malo was wet. Fresh malo, fresh kapa, all his belongings had been lost in the sea. True to their wont, the two helmsmen had gone off to warm themselves and had forgotten him.

Ku-a-Paka'a saw him sitting there and ran to his father. "E ku'u makuakane, I feel for my chief. He is cold, sitting there on his canoe. His malo is wet."

From the calabash of the winds Paka'a took out a
fresh loincloth of fine kapa, scented with maile, the same
malo he had taken with him when he left Hawai'i.

"Here is the malo for your master. Tell him your
mother made it for you. Take it to your king and ask him to
give you the wet malo he is wearing."

Ku took the loincloth down to the beach, climbed up
on the pola between the two hulls of the great canoe. Although the king had relaxed the kapu to make things
easier for his men, Ku bowed himself very low before him.

"My chief, here is fresh malo for you. Let me take
your wet one."

When Keawe-nui-a-'Umi reached to take the malo
from the boy, he looked at it for a while; then he looked
searchingly at Ku.

"This malo looks like my own."

"E ku'u ali'i, that is my malo. My mother made it for me and took care of it for the time when I should have a guest. You are the guest, my chief."

The king took off his wet malo and put on the dry. He gave the wet one to Ku to dry and care for. Ku put it on and ran with to his father.

"Here is the wet malo of my master."

"Hang it by the door. No one will enter a house made kapu by the malo of the king. You, my son, may enter and leave. Now you are dedicated. You two have worn a single garment. When the stewards come for the king's food, you will be the one to hand it to them."

But when Ku went down to the shore again, he saw that his master still sat on the canoe. The sun had passed the western gate to rest on the ocean, and the air was cool. Aloha welled up in the boy, and he went back to his father.

"My master has a malo, but he needs a covering. The evening will be cool."

Paka'a took the folded cape of fine kapa from the calabash of La'amaomao and handed it to the boy.

"Here is the cape of your master. Tell him your mother made it for you."

The cape was still fragrant with its perfume of leaves and vines. Ku wished it were his. He carried it before him with care, like an offering, and so he presented it to Keawe-nui-a-'Umi.

"O my chief, the evening here is cool. Here is my kapa for you to wear."

95

Keawe-nui-a-'Umi took the cape, shook it, and spread it out. The sweet scent of 'olapa rose from the folds.

"Boy, where did you get this kapa?"

"It is from Moloka'i here."

"But this kapa comes only from Hawai'i. It is named 'O'u-holowai-o-La'a, for the high-running water of La'a. Its making has not spread to other islands. Boy, I believe this is my own kapa. Could Paka'a be here?"

"My mother, the chiefess Hikauhi, made that kapa for me and scented it with leaves. Its name is Wailau, branching waters. It smells like the 'O'u-holowai-o-La'a. It is the best kapa we have here."

The king shook his head, finding it hard to believe, but he smiled at the boy and put on the cape.

Ku escorted the king to his father's mua, but the six chiefs of Hawai'i and their men he led to the six houses he and his father had thatched for them and supplied with food, with fresh kapa, with clean mats, with all they needed for their comfort.

When the two helmsmen saw Ku with the king they snorted and turned their backs. "He'll be steering the great canoe next!" The two laughed and laughed at their own joke. But the other retainers of the king looked on at this and said nothing.

The king's servants were without means to serve because they had lost their supplies in the sea. So that night it was Ku-a-Paka'a who waited on the king while he ate, who was there with more poi when the king wanted it, who chose the choicest bits of meat and fish for the king's bowl, who brought the bowl of fresh water to wash his fingers and the fresh towel to dry them. And it was Ku-a-Paka'a who took away the king's scraps lest they be used in a charm against his master. The king missed nothing of the boy's efforts to please him.

After the meal, Keawe-nui-a-'Umi stretched out on the pile of fine mats with some of his men. He thought back to days long ago in Hawai'i. "If Paka'a were only here! On such an evening, he would have had the 'awa bowl ready with fresh hinalea. We would drink and loosen our tongues until sleep put an end to our chatter. And then we would dream! How I long for him!"

Ku slipped out of the mua and ran to the cookhouse, where his father was resting, waiting.

"My master wants 'awa. He thinks fondly of you, e ku'u makuakane; he remembers the years of happiness with you."

Paka'a smiled. He brought out from the calabash the cup of polished coconut, the carved bowl, and the grass for straining the 'awa. He took a large piece of 'awa root and some fingers of 'awa that he had already chewed and wrapped in a piece of kapa.

"Take this 'awa to your master. Show him the root, and if he asks you to chew it, turn aside to where it is dark and put these fingers that are already chewed in the bowl with the water. Your master will compliment you. You will seem to be as quick at chewing the 'awa as I was when backbone. After you have strained the 'awa with the grass, give him the cup to drink. Then run to the beach as fast as you can and fetch two hinalea from those we chased into the pond. They will cool the bitterness of the 'awa in his throat."

Very carefully, Ku carried the cup, the bowl, and the 'awa to the king. He held out the root to Keawe-nui-a-'Umi.

"Here is your 'awa, my chief."

Keawe-nui-a-'Umi eyed the large piece of root. "You chew it for me."

Ku turned quickly to a dark corner of the house, added the chewed fingers of 'awa to the water in the bowl, strained the mixture, and offered the cup of 'awa to his chief. Then he ran to the fish pond on the beach to fetch the sweet fish; they were still alive and cool when he put them on the king's plate.

"Mahalo nui. Boy, you certainly are quick! You serve like one who has lived with a king."

Ku smiled his thanks and went to sit in the corner of the house. Keawe-nui-a-'Umi drank, and the 'awa and the care of the boy eased him after the strain of the day, and soothed his sense of loss. He felt happy once more. While Ku watched, the king and his men slipped into sleep.

When he was sure all the men slept, Ku stole out of the mua and back to his father. He opened slightly the wind calabash of La'amaomao, and the winds that had gone off rushed back and tore up the calm night. While the weary guests slept, the wind and storm raged over Moloka'i. And so it was for many days. Though they never knew their host, Keawe-nui-a-'Umi and his men were captives as well as guests of Paka'a and his son Ku for nearly a month.

CHAPTER TWELVE

One morning during the windy month, while the others lay low under cover, Paka'a picked up his ti leaf rain cape and called to his son Ku.

"Say, you who sleep, let's go look for a hollow tree."

"A hollow tree for what?" Ku tied his rain cape around his shoulders.

"A tree to hold the food for my revenge on my enemies."

The two searched in the forest until they found a large, straight tree that was hollow. They cleaned it out inside and dragged it down to the house of Ho'olehua, Ku's grandfather.

"Now let's find a large stone."

"A stone for what?"

"A stone to anchor the chief's canoe for my revenge on my enemies."

They found a large stone of basalt and ground a groove in it to hold fast a rope. Then Paka'a said to the boy, "Soon the chief and his men will have eaten all the food we set aside for them and what they could save from the swamping. They will come to you for food. Give them the six fields of cane and the six patches of potatoes we planted in the uplands, but ask them to leave for you the small potatoes. Those they should peel and dry. You must take the small potatoes to your grandfather, who will store them in the hollow tree. Then put in dry fish, water gourds, the palm leaves we carried down from the uplands, and strong rope for the anchor. The stone and the tree, these will be your bundles. If the king asks you to sail back with him to Hawai'i, you will go, but only if you can take on board with you your bundles."

Paka'a then sketched out to Ku his plan for revenge. Ku listened and stored it all in his mind.

The plan began to work almost immediately. At the end of the month of storms, one of the chiefs sent word to the king that their food was gone. By now Keawe-nui-a-'Umi was wont to ask Ku for what he needed.

"Go to the boy. Perhaps he has food."

The helmsmen, who stood nearby, objected. "O king, you give the boy too much importance. We are many. We could take his food. You pay him too much honor."

101

"One fishes where one is certain there are fish. The boy's thought is for others as well as for himself. He wears his honor like a man and the son of a chief, as we should."

The messenger brought Ku to Keawe-nui-a-'Umi.

"Boy, I sent for you because we have no food left and my people are hungry. Is there food?"

"My chief, there is food. Six chiefs of Hawai'i came with you. Six small fields of cane and six small patches of potatoes grow in the uplands. Send your men to pull the cane and dig the potatoes. But tell them not to leave the small ones. They are to bring them all down, large and small. It will be their only chance to go up there for food."

"But how can six small fields of cane and six small patches of potatoes feed all my men?"

"Oh, those plants up there get lonely. They like to see people. The more they see come to pull and dig, the more they will bear." Ku had already seen that some of the king's men must have had lazy fathers.

So some went and some stayed. But when the chiefs and their men climbed to the uplands, they could not believe their eyes. The potato and cane fields stretched as far as a man could see, as far as a man could run and not drop. The chiefs sent for those who had stayed behind to get themselves up there and dig.

They pulled the sugar cane and dug the sweet potatoes, large and small, and took down as much as they could carry. On the shore they lighted their imu. When they had roasted the potatoes, the men offered some of them to Lono.

102

"O Lono! God of the husbandman,
  Give life to the land!"

Then Ku said to them, "Take the large potatoes for yourselves; leave the small ones for me."

"What? Not so. You must have some large ones too."

"No. You must keep the large ones, but peel the small ones and dry them in the sun."

103

"Why so, boy?"

"Don't you thatch your house when the rain is far off? In a short time you will eat all the potatoes in the uplands. When the fine days come, then you will sail. Leave me the small potatoes and I shall have food to eat when I plant more crops after you have cleaned out my fields."

"Say! He's a keiki ho'opi!" But those nicknamed stingy did not want. The men laughed and did what Ku asked.

Then they went to the beach and waded into the sea, beating the water with their feet until they chased the small fish into a net. No one went hungry.

Ku dried his fish in the sun and took all his dried potatoes and fish to his grandfather to store in the tree. He carried the palm leaves, he carried the rope. He and his grandfather stored everything away in the tree, his bundle.

CHAPTER THIRTEEN

When Keawe-nui-a-'Umi set sail from Hawai'i with his flock of winged canoes to look for his man Paka'a, he gave word to those who stayed behind that he would be gone a month. But now a month had gone by. The people of Hawai'i gave up their king for lost. With weeping and wailing, with prayers and with ceremonies, with chanting of dirges, they mourned his death.

Meanwhile on Moloka'i, in the hearts of the seekers and voyagers, aloha welled up for those they had left, and they too grieved. They longed to go home.

Now that his bundles were ready, Ku-a-Paka'a closed the wind calabash of La'amaomao, and the calm days came once more, the days when the fisherman's line is never dry. Now Ku urged the chiefs, "Make fast the lashings on your canoes. See, it is calm; the stormy months are past. Now you can go home." The boy was everywhere, stirring up the men to get ready to leave. "Rig the canoes! Then sleep until your eyes are rested. A royal trip is coming up. Get ready!"

Men and birds alike fall in line behind the one who knows where he goes. The chiefs bade their men rig the canoes, renew the torn lashings, load the water gourds, the poi, push the canoes out into the water and moor them. In the very early morning of the next day, when the fish of the Milky Way had turned toward the western heavens, they would sail.

The men fell on their mats like stones that night before the long paddling. But their eyes had closed only a
short time when Ku-a-Paka‘a rose, drew a kapa about his
shoulders, and went out into the starry night. He ran to the
houses where the six chiefs of Hawai‘i slept and called:

"E ala! E ala! Arise!
  The night is spent! Ua kulu ka po!
  Gone the weariness, the ache, the soreness,
  Gone the dizziness from rigging the canoes.
  E ala! Arise!
  The morning star is in the sky,
  The star at the end of the land, O!
  Arise! Move! Let's sail!"

Now, the man whose duty it was to wake the chiefs
was Kiauau. The sleepy men grunted, "What's got into
Kiauau? Can't he tell time? It's night!" And they rolled
over.

"Wait! Maybe Kiauau has fears and would wake us."
Again they heard the chant:

"E ala! E ala! Arise!"

Some of them pulled themselves up, but when they
came out into the starlight and found instead of the man
Kiauau the slim boy with the big lungs, they were annoyed.

"Auwe noho‘i e! So it is you! Boy, you have a fine
voice, but where is your head? We had just begun to sleep,
and here you come telling us the morning star is up!"

In their houses the six chiefs of Hawai'i hugged their mats, letting themselves be swept again and again back into the tides of sleep. When the eyes had had their rest and the fish had turned, that would be time enough to sail.

So Ku called to them by district. Would pride rouse them?

"Arise, Kona, land of the calm sea...
    Arise, Hamakua of the high-flying highroads...
    Make a move, Kohala of the solid heights...
    Arise, Hilo of the adz-like rain...
    Arise, O Puna, fragrant with hala...
    Arise, great Ka-'u, the windy land...
    Sail, the small canoes,
    Sail, the tall masts,
    The smooth-sliding canoes of the chiefs,
    Sail!"

When the chiefs heard their districts named, they guessed that the king had sent word and that the chant was for them. Grumbling and stiff and rubbing their eyes, they sat up. But they did not come out of their houses. They waited to be asked again.

So this time Ku called them by name.

"E ala! It is day! It is bright!
    E ala! Get moving, Kohala,
    Land of Wahilani."

Wahilani stumbled out into the starlight. "This boy is sending us away!"

107

"E ala! E ala!
The young wind is stirring—
E ala! Hamakua,
Land of Wanu'a."

Wanu'a heard. "Let's get up then. Sleep is pau for this night!"

Ku went on to the next house.

"E ala! E ala!
The light wind that brings the small bait fish,
It lifts.
The lehua blossom unfolds under the foot
    of the rain.
E ala! E ala! Hilo,
Land of Kulukulu'a."

Kulukulu'a heard his land, his name. He got up and roused his men. "Say, you who sleep, wake up, we sail! Here comes the call!" But when he saw that it was Ku-a-Paka'a doing the calling, he said, "The eyes had just closed, and this fellow calls them to open. He's sending us off!"

"E ala! It is day!
  The sun is up over Kumukahi...
E ala! Arise, Puna,
  Land of Hua'a."

Hua'a called to his men, "Wake up, you who sleep. Don't go rolling yourselves up in the bed kapa. There's the call!"

The men of Puna got up. But when Hua'a saw Ku, he said, "Auwe noho'i e! This is strange. This boy wants us gone! Say, you young trickster, who said the sun rises at night?"

Ku answered back, "The native son of Kumukahi. He naps after sunset, rises before midnight, sets off in his canoe to fish 'opelu. So the sun is up at night, isn't it?"

The men laughed in spite of their annoyance.

Ku went on to the next house.

"Arise, Ka-'u, windy land
  Of the whistling trades.
E ala! Arise, Ka-'u,
  Land of Makaha."

109

Makaha heard. "Wake up, you sleepers. It's our turn to be called." The men got up and got ready to sail. Makaha said to Ku, "My land is a windy land, but there the men stay put; only the rubbish is blown away. Here the men are blown away. They can't even get a good night's sleep!"

"The wind of your land is a tale-bearing wind. There is no land with winds like those of Moloka'i. They knock the houses down. You are safer if you get up and come out."

"Wise words to Makaha!" The other men laughed.

Ku went on to the last of the chiefs.

"E ala! Arise!
Awake, men of Kona!
Kona, calmed by the gentle wind—
E ala! Kona!
Land of 'Ehu."

'Ehu had heard the other chiefs being called, for the houses were close together. When he heard his name, he called his people: "Up, Kona men. At least the eyes have winked. Not too bad!"

But when they straggled out into the night and looked up at the night sky, they said, "How, boy? The fish have not turned and here you get us up. You must be driving us off."

But the boy had been right before. He was probably right this time. The men were boarding the canoes when a messenger from the king, awakened by the noise, ran down to the beach, telling them to sail west toward Ka'ula and wait near Leahi.

One by one the canoes set off over the pale water, the men grumbling over their short sleep, peering into the sky for a sign. They all left, the single paddlers, the canoes with two, with three, with four—all of them left, and the only canoe that stayed was the great canoe of Keawe-nui-a-'Umi.

The tide was high. The canoes slipped over the reef with no trouble. Once out on the open sea, the paddlers set their sails and paddled to the west, toward Ka'ula, where their king would find Paka'a. They left the black hills of Moloka'i behind them. When they were off Leahi, on O'ahu, they hove to, to wait for Keawe-nui-a-'Umi.

But the push of the soft wind, the rhythm of the waters, lulled the men who had slept so little, and they nodded. Soon the drone of snores mingled with the swish of foam against the sides of the canoes.

"Sleep then!" The sailing masters lowered the sails before they should lose paddles and sleepers as well, and they too drifted into sleep, while the canoes themselves drifted into the wide ocean current.

When the undersides of the small clouds turned pink and the sky paled, the sailing masters of the chiefs' canoes awoke and set up their sails to be ready for the king when he came. But when the sky was light and the mists cleared, they knew that the mountains they saw were not those of Oʻahu or Maui, but of Hawaiʻi.

So the great fleet landed at Kawaihae. While the men were sorry for the sake of their king, joy and aloha flooded up in their hearts at the thought of seeing their wives and children. When the canoes landed, men far off could hear the cries and the weeping of those who rushed into the water to greet whom they loved. Aloha! Aloha nui loa! And the joy overflowed when the people of Hawaiʻi learned that their king lived.

CHAPTER FOURTEEN

When the last of the six canoes of the chiefs sailed off in the night, Ku went up to his father's house, threw himself on a mat, and slept till dawn. The sky had paled when he woke up, went outside, and called in a loud voice:

"E ala! Arise!
E ala! Arise! Arise, Hawai'i,
Great land of Kane!"

The call awoke the paddlers of the great canoe, who stirred themselves and took their paddles down to the beach. Keawe-nui-a-'Umi awoke and sent a messenger to fetch Ku before him. The king was loath to leave behind the boy who was now so useful to him. Aloha warmed his smile when the messenger appeared with the tall child.

"I sent for you, boy, so that we two can sail to Ka'ula to look for Paka'a."

"O my chief, I cannot go with you. Who will look after my old father, who is deaf?"

"You sail with me, boy. Your father won't have any trouble. You'll be back here in a short while. Your father won't have time to miss you."

"But, my chief, I have another problem. I could go with you, but I have bundles that I must have with me. If you will take my bundles on board your canoe, then I can sail with you."

"Yes, let's sail together, boy. Send some men to get your bundles."

But when the two men went with Ku to the house of Ho'olehua, they found a tree almost as long as the hulls of the great canoe. Ku pointed to it. "Here is one of my bundles. You can take it to the king's canoe and then come back for the other."

"Auwe noho'i e! What a joke! You said you had a couple of bundles. You didn't say you had a tree!"

But the king had given his word to Ku; so the men pulled and strained and finally heaved the tree to their shoulders and carried it down to the great canoe.

The paddlers and helmsmen saw it coming.

"What's that tree for?"

"Oh, this is just the bundle of the boy. The king told him he could take it on board. The king won't sail without the boy. The boy won't sail without his bundles. So give us a hand!"

The two helmsmen turned away in disgust, but with the help of the paddlers, the men managed to slide the tree on to the pola. Then they returned to Ku. He pointed to a large stone with a groove in the middle. "Here's this little bundle. You two take it and put it on the king's canoe."

"Well, boy, you're a funny one. Here the bundle you sail with is a rock. I've worked at court all my life till I am gray. I've never seen a single chief sail with a bundle like this!"

Ku-a-Paka'a said, "Some women came here with you people."

"Why talk about women? We're talking about a rock!"

"Well, women weigh down canoes too."

"They do that, boy!" The men grinned, thinking of the portly chiefesses who had almost swamped their canoes before they got started.

"And they don't work, either."

The men shook their heads. With great effort they picked up the stone and carried it down to the chief's canoe.

"What's that stone for?"

"Oh, this is one more bundle of the boy. If the chief had known about these bundles, he wouldn't have been so quick to say they could come."

"Children of Kaluako'i have large bundles!" commented the people who had come down to the beach to see the chief sail. "Those bundles could sink a canoe!" And now the canoe did sit a good bit lower in the water.

Once Ku saw that his bundles were surely on board, he ran back to the house of his mother. Aloha! And then to the cookhouse, where his father had stayed out of the way of the visitors.

"E ku'u makuakane, my bundles are on."

Paka'a took out the wind calabash of La'amaomao, placed it in the boy's hands, and looked hard into his son's eyes, a look that was blessing, that was trust, that was hope. Ku felt himself grow a hand taller with that look.

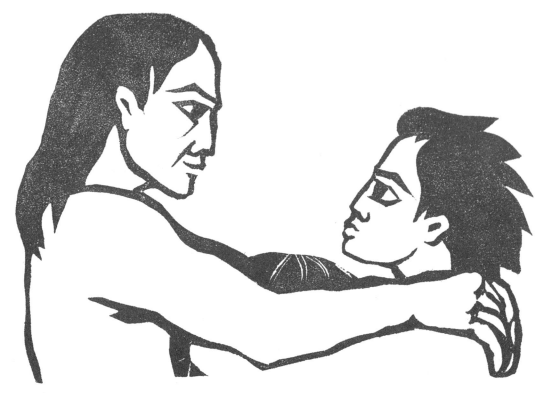

"Go, Ku-a-Paka'a. Do not look back, but remember!"

"'Ae. I go young to do your bidding, Father. If I die, it will not matter. I will have done what is to be done. But if I live, your enemies will die. You will be avenged."

How could the words hold a life, a heart, and its hope? O aloha! The boy left his father like an unbarbed spear sped to its goal.

Ku carried the calabash in its net to the house where the chief stayed. "My chief, my bundles are on board. Let's sail."

The chief and his men stood up from the mats where they had been waiting, and the group went down to the beach, Ku by the side of his master. He did not look back, but he could almost feel the yearning that followed him. Truly he was Ku, standing in the place of Paka'a.

When the paddlers saw the boy coming, they began to shout, "Here come more bundles of Kaluako'i!"

The chief and his men boarded the canoe, Keawe-nui-a-'Umi taking the high seat on the pola. Ku sat in front of the men. The two steersmen were at the rear. As soon as all were in place, they set sail, just as the sun broke free of the point of Kamalo. At that moment the mists that drifted off the mountains rose and a rainbow arched over the waters. A high chief sailed!

Ku was silent. He remembered his first sight of the great canoe, a blaze appearing out of the sunrise. Now he, Ku-a-Paka'a, was a part of that glitter, was near that blaze. But at the heart of the light was a human heart. Ku thought of the words his father had told him his grandfather Ku-a-Nu'uanu had said before he died: "Listen to his small wish, listen to his great demand..." The small wish—that would be easy, because his father had trained him well. And the great demand? Wasn't that to protect the king from who might harm him? Wasn't that to love him? Ku sighed. The morning was almost too full.

The helmsmen set the sail to catch the Kona wind and the trades and they set the course to the west. The paddlers dipped their paddles in steady rhythm, and the great canoe flew.

After his first moment of awe, Ku looked around to see how the helmsmen braced the great steering paddles at the stern.

"You steer well."

The two men snorted and would not notice the boy.

"Let me hold one of your paddles," he asked, "just to hold it. I like the way you do it."

"Why should you hold one of our paddles? Don't you know we are helmsmen here?" The two men turned their backs on the boy and did not know they turned their backs on their future.

They sailed west, away from Moloka'i, past the lee of O'ahu, sailed across the Ka'ie'iewaho channel, and soon could see Kaua'i. Ku thought, "The land I see is the land of my grandmother La'amaomao and her mother La'amaomao before her, and may her mana fill me!" When the great canoe had passed by Koloa and was outside Waimea on the way to Ka'ula, Ku-a-Paka'a opened the calabash of the winds.

The winds of Kaua'i and the wind of Ka'ula heard the call from the mouth of the gourd. The canoe that had seemed so big in the harbor was now a shell on the heaving ocean. For the winds swept it out to sea away from the land. The sky turned black, and the mouths of the waves choked on their own foam.

As the green-black hawk, the 'iwa, swoops down on the white tern to thieve its fish, then dips, tosses, worries its prey until it is limp and lifeless, so the black storm clouds hovered over the canoe of Keawe-nui-a-'Umi, tirelessly tossing, playing, waiting for it to tire, to give up its life. The black bird begged the bones of the chief and his men.

The paddlers paddled, the bailers bailed, fighting the fury of the storm. But from the effort, from the cold that numbed, the rain that stung, from the wind that cut like an adz, from the sea that poured in from before, from behind, from that side, from this side, the men weakened.

Now they could hardly see the coast of Kaua'i. The king called back to the helmsmen, "What are we to do?"

The two strove to brace their steering paddles to steady the canoe. They did not answer their king. The king asked once more, and again the two did not answer.

Keawe-nui-a-'Umi turned to Ku. "Boy, then I ask you the question. What of this storm? What shall we do?" And by this question, all the men on the great canoe knew that the king had given over the command of the great canoe to the boy.

"My chief, I have this rock. It could be an anchor to hold the canoe. We must not lose sight of land."

Ku took out the straw plug from one end of the hollow tree, thrust in his arm, and pulled out the long rope of olona. He tied it around the middle rock. With the help of the men, he pushed the rock into the sea. The anchor held. They now could wait out the end of the storm.

At the heart of the fury, the king was calm. He was with the boy who knew his way through storms. So much did Keawe-nui-a-'Umi now trust Ku-a-Paka'a.

Ku looked at the men, cold and spent. Their hair hung in strings, their teeth chattered, they were numb enough to lose their grip on the paddles, on the canoe itself. He reached into the tree again and brought out the fan-palm

119

leaves that he and his father had brought down from the uplands. To the chief and each of his men, except the two helmsmen, Ku gave a large leaf to fend off the rain. Hatred flashed from the eyes of the helmsmen, but the faces of the men who knew them were masks. No one offered a leaf.

The men slapped their flanks and their thighs with their hands. Ku thrust his arm once more into the log and pulled out the dried sweet potatoes and the dried fish. He fed his chief and his men, except the two helmsmen. When the men's stomachs warmed with the food and they began to hope, Ku gave them water, all but the two helmsmen. No one offered them food. No one offered water.

Ho'okele-i-Hilo and Ho'okele-i-Puna now knew they would never see Hilo and Puna again. It was too late to regret the untrue word said and the true word unsaid, the cruel deed done and the kind deed undone. They were no longer the king's helmsmen.

The two thought back to the prophecy of the boy: "You two will die in the ocean in the plain sight of all." They were not afraid, they did not doubt. But they knew that a mana worked that was more powerful than lies or truth, than cruelty or kindness. They bowed to the mana.

Ku heard the two men slapping their bodies, trying to pound blood through their stiff skins. They were blue with cold, but they said nothing of their suffering. Ku was torn in his heart between pity for the misery of the men and the prod of his father's command. He felt himself a boy in a man's storm.

Not long after, the men at the stern heard a splash. A paddler called out, "Ho'okele-i-Hilo has fallen into the sea!" Before anyone could move, there was another splash. This time no one called. No one leaped into the churning sea. No one spoke.

And so the two enemies of Paka'a died as they would have seen him die in the sea of Alenuihaha, when they followed him from Hawai'i.

CHAPTER FIFTEEN

"You are avenged, O my father!" Once the two helmsmen who had wronged Paka'a had slipped into the long sleep, Ku closed the calabash of the winds. Heavens and sea became calm once more.

The king had seen. Trips like these in the great canoe, free of the rigid ways of the court, showed him his men for what they were. When the two helmsmen had slipped off the stern of the canoe, the masks of the paddlers could not hide their feelings of relief.

Keawe-nui-a-'Umi turned to Ku. "Boy, my sailing masters are gone. Not one of our men has their skill. Tell me, can you handle the stern of the canoe?"

"I can try, O my chief," said Ku, and he moved to the place of one of the two steersmen. He asked the men to pull up the anchor; he picked up one of the great steering paddles and set it in the water. The life of the canoe was in his hands.

"Boy, now that it is calm once more, let us sail to Ka'ula to seek Paka'a. Can you bring us back safe to Hawai'i?"

"'Ae, e ku'u ali'i. We shall find Paka'a."

The sun broke through the clouds and warmed the spent men. They nodded and drowsed and soon took their paddles into the canoe. Then they slept.

When Ku saw that all, including his chief, were asleep, he turned the bow of the canoe toward O'ahu. He opened the wind calabash of La'amaomao and a fair western wind blew at their stern. Passing to the south of O'ahu, Ku set

the course to go below the red rock of Kaho'olawe. All the
day the men slept, sickened and stupefied by the sun, as if
under a charm. When they awoke, they felt the cool night
air, they felt the wind at the stern, and thought they must
be near Ka'ula. But when the day broke and great Mauna
Kea floated before them above the mist, they knew they
were near home.

"There's Hawai'i!"

Gladness rippled over the men like a breeze over tall
grass. They burned to see the faces of their wives, their
children. The king was startled to see the long slopes of
Kawaihae. He had failed to find Paka'a, but he was grate-
ful to the boy for the safe trip home. Keawe-nui-a-'Umi
would look for Paka'a at a less stormy season.

As they neared shore, Ku-a-Paka'a looked at the faces
of the men, bright with eagerness and hope. He felt suddenly alone, a stranger who looks on at the preparations
for a feast, but knows that he will not be asked to eat.

123

From far off over the waters floated the high cries of the children who would wade splashing into the sea to greet their fathers when the canoe landed.

"Ei nei. How many have love for their children?" Ku asked of his uncle, who stood near.

"What of that, boy?" said Lapakahoe. He looked into Ku's face, but Ku was looking off toward shore.

"Being left behind when the canoe is beached."

"Why would you be left behind with the canoe? Your chief will not forget you, boy. Because of you these bones live."

But Ku had guessed all too well. As soon as the great canoe touched land, the chiefs and men leaped onto the sand. They rushed arms open to greet their wives, their children, their parents, their friends, with weeping and laughing. The haku mele chanted with joy the name of their king, the names of his chiefs; and the high chief and his priests and attendants swept off to the court. The people ran there, they ran here, drawing the canoe up on the beach, telling their friends of the storms, of the stay on Moloka'i. From their homes they brought food for the feast; they brought pigs and dogs for the sacrifice, to give thanks for the return of their chief alive.

After the chants, after the weeping, the people went to their homes with their own, and the boy was forgotten. Ku waited by the canoes on the beach. Surely someone would fetch him, someone would ask him. The smoke from the imus rose, and the odor of roast pig made him swallow hard. But no one came to fetch him. No one came to ask him.

The men thought surely the chief would take care of the boy who had saved their bones. The chief thought all would be eager to invite the boy who had cared for them, had fed them, had saved them. Each thought the other would act; so no one acted. And Ku was left on the beach with the canoes.

As evening came on, Ku knew that the people had forgotten him; so he cleaned out the hulls and the pola of the great canoe. He would stay there. The great canoe of the chief, that had sailed out of the eyeball of the sun, became home for Ku-a-Paka'a. He had his tree, the water, his dried fish, his dried sweet potatoes, which he ate until his throat

was dried. And so he lived, without friends, for several days until the malolo season, caring for the canoe of the king, listening, biding his time, waiting his chance.

One evening as Ku sat on the sand, with his back to one of the canoe hulls, he overheard the head fisherman, a man appointed by Ho'okele-i-Hilo and Ho'okele-i-Puna, ordering his men to ready the canoes for a drive for flying fish in the morning.

Ku slept as usual under the pola of the great canoe, but at dawn he got up and walked along the beach to where the people beached their canoes. Two men were tightening lashings on their canoe.

"Do you two go out for malolo?"

"'Ae. What of that?"

"I wonder if you can take with you a boy."

"No. Our canoe would draw too much water. We two will go."

"But every canoe needs a bailer. If I go with you, your share of fish will not come to me. I know this type of fishing. If the catch is large, each paddler gets a ka'au; if the catch is small, each gets four. You will not lose." Ku spoke as if he knew.

"'Ae. Let's sail together then."

The boy helped tighten the lashings and lift the canoe into the water. The three boarded it and paddled off with the fishing fleet. The canoe skimmed along.

When the sky had lost the red dawn-glow and the sun was about to appear, the canoe fleet had a load of malolo. Each man drew forty fish, and the canoes headed for shore.

While the three took their time about paddling in, Ku saw a large canoe with six men in it. He knew the canoe of the two men was fleet. "What about racing that canoe there?"

"Auwe noho'i e! Six men can beat three. How can we win?" said one.

"Then you change to that canoe and we two will race the seven of you," said Ku.

"'A'ole loa! I can't see myself racing with you, boy, against all those seven men!" said the other man.

"Then the two of you change to that canoe and there'll be eight of you. We'll race and the ka'au of malolo will be the wager. If you reach land first, you get my fish. If I reach land first, I get yours."

"Is that so? We'll ask those men."

"'Ae," agreed the six men. "Let's find out what a strong paddler is this fire-eater." The men were sure of winning.

When the two had climbed into the canoe with the six, they said, "Say, boy, let's put your fish in this canoe."

Ku almost smiled at the men's guile. It was just like the race his father had won when he was a boy. The tale-bearing winds keep blowing.

"No. I think you should put your fish in mine. If I win, you people might not want to give up your fish. If you win, there are eight of you. What have you to fear from me?"

True. What could they fear from an unknown boy? So they paddled the canoes close together, and the men scooped their fish into the boy's canoe.

One of the men muttered, with his head bent, "We make trouble for ourselves. Why wait till we land to take the fish? We will win."

"Maybe so," said Ku, "but I have heard old men say, 'The large hau tree is grooved by the small hau.'"

This answer annoyed the men. They paddled along together. Ku could see that the eight men paddled evenly, that side, this side. Their canoe flew.

At a point, Ku called, "Let's race!"

"'Ae." And when the canoes were even, "'Oia!" Off they leaped with the first thrust of the paddles.

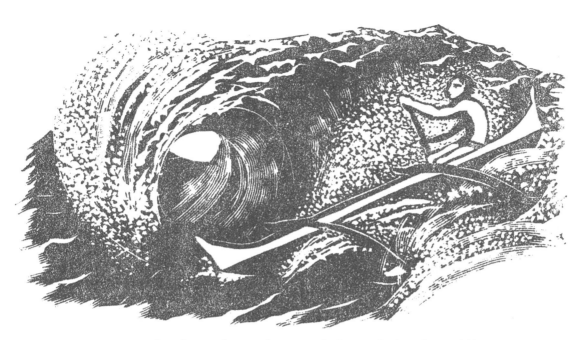

From the first, the eight men left Ku behind. Paddle as he would he could see that he could never beat such strong paddlers. He thought of the sail of his father when he was a boy in such a race. But he had no sail. Now, if a huge wave were to lift him in, then he could land first. He thought of his great-grandmother, La'amaomao.

"O mother of my father's mother,
Great La'amaomao,
Send me, send me a wind.
May the waves rise from the east,
So the son of your grandson can land!
And you and I will eat malolo together!"

The wind lifted, and a huge roller curled toward Ku's canoe. When he saw the swells tower behind him, Ku began paddling furiously. Then when he caught the crest of the

129

wave and the stern of the canoe rose, he braced the paddle and let the wave carry him in. He did not doubt. He was not afraid. Ku-a-Paka'a was in the hands of his.

When the eight men saw the huge rollers behind them, they thought they would be swamped and their canoe would be smashed. They stopped paddling and held the canoe back from entering the channel for landing. When they saw Ku flying in toward shore, they shouted,

"Say!
The boy is landing!
He lands!"

"What I worry about is the canoe. He doesn't care. It's not his. All he wants is our fish!" said one of the men.

The wave cast Ku's canoe far up on the sand. He lifted it to a place where the sea could not claim it, took out the fish, and hid them in the hulls of the great canoe. Then he sat down on the sand to wait for the others.

One wave passed, then another, then a third. Finally the sea calmed once more, and the eight men headed their canoe toward the beach and landed. They called to Ku.

"Where are the fish?"

"There are no fish. I gave the whole lot away. I knew I had won."

The men had been out in the cold from early dawn to daybreak. They, the king's fishermen, had lost a race to a mere boy. Now, with no fish to take home, they were furious. In a group they planted themselves before Ku-a-Paka'a, and their faces were black clouds.

"What do you say we race again? The waves helped you. Had you paddled all the way, the race and the fish would have been ours."

"As you wish," said Ku. "The race was to reach land first."

"Will you race?" The faces of the men were storms.

"I'll race," said Ku, "but I have nothing to wager."

"One wager we all have—our bones. If you beat us, we die. If we beat you, you die."

Ku was in heavy surf. "Why wager the bones? I don't wish the bodies to die. If you beat me, I have no friends here, no one will grieve. I am only a nameless child. But you, you have wives, and children, and friends to weep and mourn your death. Why not wager our wealth? There's my wealth." Ku pointed to the double canoe of the king that he had been cleaning and tending for several days now.

"Auwe noho'i e! That isn't your canoe! That is the canoe of the king!"

"The king rode with me, but I care for the canoe. For now it is mine. If it belonged to some other person, would not that person care for it?"

The men were shocked that the boy would dare. Ku was a little surprised at himself.

"We don't want the canoe. We wager the bones."

"'Ae. But should I win and you join the heap of the dead, know: the wager was your wish, not mine."

The boy's spirit angered the men. "'Ae. We'll race at Ka-'u in the long canoes. The one to lose will be cooked in an imu."

"'Ae. Agreed," said Ku.

Ku was up against hard men, and he knew it. His father had told him of the eight fishermen appointed by Ho'okele-i-Hilo and Ho'okele-i-Puna, their friends. They had pushed the fishermen of Paka'a from their place and from their canoes. Ka-'u was the land of the long winds and the high surfs. The canoes would be the racing canoes of six fathoms, heavy for a strong man.

When the rest of the malolo fleet pulled in, the people went home and boasted of the nameless boy who had won a race over Keawe-nui-a-'Umi's fishermen. The news of the race that was and the race that would be sped all over the island. But no one at court imagined that the unknown boy was the boy of Moloka'i who had saved their lives.

CHAPTER SIXTEEN

From all the six districts of Hawai'i, men, women, and children thronged to Ka-'u for the race.

"A race!
There will be a race!
A boy who does not give his name
Will race the king's fishermen,
The wager the bones!"

The eight fishermen and Ku paddled their canoes around the southern point of the island to Ka-'u, land of the black sands, land of the white water. When the people arrived, Ku saw the wealth they had brought to wager— a pig about to litter, plump dogs, bird feathers from the uplands, a damp type of kapa, a strong fishline, an adz, a fine calabash. Many were on the side of the eight fishermen, some risking all they had; for the sport, a few put their hopes on the lone boy in the long canoe.

133

The night before the race, the eight fishermen slept on the beach near their canoe. A way off, near the canoe that had been loaned him, slept Ku. In the morning, the fishermen were up early, piling up rocks for the imu of the loser, gathering wood, digging the pit, setting the wood to light as soon as they had won the race.

From his canoe, Ku watched them. In his heart he said a prayer to Ku and his wife Lea, gods of the canoe, gods of his fathers.

"O Ku of the sacred ocean,
O Lea,
Here is your child, Ku-a-Paka'a.
Keep him safe!"

Onlookers helped the boy lift the heavy canoe down to the edge of the water. The eight men lifted theirs. Then they called out to Ku, "The imu waits. Shall we sail?"

"'A'ole. Not yet," said Ku. "We need a couple of surfboards."

"Why surfboards? We race in canoes."

"If we paddle to a set point and come back, let's have one final test, in the surf. If I land first, I'll take a surfboard and ride four waves. If you land first, one of you will do the same. Should I lose, I die."

"'Ae. Agreed." The men called for the surfboards to be placed on the sand. But in their haste they did not say which wave to ride—the wave that broke on the sand, or the wave that broke far out.

Ku-a-Paka'a boarded his canoe, the eight boarded theirs, and they paddled out to sea, away from the crowd gathered on the beach.

After a time Ku looked back. He could no longer see the white foam break on the black shore.

"I say!" he called to the others. "Shall we turn back from here? The single paddler will lose if we go farther."

"No. We'll start in when the sea hides the houses." The men were firm, and they did not stop paddling.

"Do eight stones break so easily? Why fear me? You could win without trying if we had started from where the big waves break. But you bail out already. Now the ones to pity are your parents, wives, and children!"

The eight kept on paddling, thinking to tire the boy. When the houses on shore were lost behind the swells, they called to Ku, "Here we are. Here we start."

"'Ae."

Ku turned his canoe around and lined it up with the others. When they were even, the men called out, "Ready! Paddle!"

The eight men and Ku plunged their paddles deep, and the canoes leaped off. The men were so eager, each tried to outdo the other; their canoe shot ahead. But Ku saw that they were not used to racing. They set no beat for their strokes. Instead of dipping together with a deep thrust, they held their paddles high and brought up foam that the wind blew away. Their shallow strokes made a current that eddied from the stern of their canoe.

Ku paddled furiously, brought his canoe into that swift current, and to hold it there, braced his paddle. The faster the eight men paddled, the faster Ku's canoe followed, towed by the current in the wake of the other. The last of the eight looked back and saw the bow of Ku's canoe right behind them.

"Paddle! Paddle!
Paddle for your lives!
Here am I right behind you!"

The men did not answer. They put forth all they had.

When the people on shore saw the canoe of the eight come in sight beyond the far waves, they shouted, "Say! Here comes the canoe of the fishermen! Here they come!" They cheered their side and eyed the wagers on the sand.

"Auwe noho'i e! Where is the canoe of the boy? Aloha 'ino!" cried others, chilled with fear for the child. The canoes were still too far off. No one could see Ku's canoe just behind the other. The smoke of the imu hung over the crowd and darkened the morning air.

Now the men strained. Sweat poured down their backs and smarted their eyes, their arms ached, their breath tore at their lungs. Some sagged over their paddles.

When Ku saw the men drained of their strength, he spurted his canoe out of the current, and darted his bow up even with theirs. In a frenzy now, the men plunged their paddles, that way, this way, but there was no power in the plunge. Ku's canoe shot out ahead.

"Auwe noho'i e!
There is the boy!
The boy leads!"

Ku's heart sang when he heard the shouts and cries from the shore.

"O my father,
You are avenged!"

The canoe of Ku-a-Paka'a skimmed over the last waters through the shore surfs to the sand. He leaped out, grabbed a koa board, and dashed into the water. Throwing himself on the board, he paddled out with his hands, then turned, caught the roller, rising to his feet as he slid down the clear green slope of the curling wave.

"Say! A gannet swoops over the waters!"

Those for the boy were beside themselves, yelling and shouting. Those for the eight sulked, sat down hard on the ground, clutched at the sand with their fists.

Wave after wave Ku rode, and now the glee of the crowd burst forth in the shouts.

"The boy has won! The boy has won!"

The eight men gaped to see the canoe of Ku-a-Paka'a glide up on the sand before theirs. They were stunned to see that he rode the shore surfs and not the waves far out. But they had not said which wave. They did not argue.

While the crowd circled the boy, the eight men landed without a word, and sat down on the sand. They saw the people pick up their wagers. They saw the smoke from the imu and thought of their wives, their children, and their friends, who would weep a bundle of tears. They did not doubt. They were not afraid. But they bent their heads.

138

Runners dashed off to spread the news of the race through the countryside, to the settlements along the coast, in the valleys, to the court.

"The unknown boy has won the race with eight of the king's fishermen! The wager, the bones!"

The people felt the first stir of change. Their king had the long yellow teeth of age. His helmsmen, his favorites, had not come back from his last voyage, and now the fishermen they favored were to be roasted in an imu. The wager of the men was foolish. But to win a race with all the odds against him, the boy must have eaten brains!

When an attendant at court heard the news, he ran to the king.

"I have news!"

"What is your news!"

"There was a race!"

The king bent forward. "Who raced?"

"Eight of your fishermen raced with an unknown boy."

"The wager?"

"The bones. Roasting in an imu."

"Who won the race?"

"The boy, my chief."

"Where are my men?"

"They squat on the sand and listen to the weeping of theirs."

"Auwe!" The king bent his head. The men were good fishermen. He thought for a moment; his face sharpened. "Perhaps he is a young boy?"

"'Ae. Just a young boy."

"Auwe! If the boy is the one who sailed with us, those men will not escape. Go find the boy and bring him to me."

The servant found Ku-a-Paka'a still on the beach at Ka-'u. "The king orders you to go before him."

"'Ae. Let's go." Would the king remember him? Ku wondered.

When they arrived at Kawaihae and entered the pa of the court, Ku saw the white kapa ball of the kapu and stopped short, not daring further. But when Keawe-nui-a-'Umi saw standing there the boy who had cared for him, who had saved his life, remorse and aloha burst over him in a flood. He wept that he had forgotten the care, had neglected the giver.

The king made a sign for the kapu standard to be taken away, and for the boy to come to him. When Ku came before him, bent very low, Keawe-nui-a-'Umi lifted him, enfolded him in his arms, and rubbed the boy's nose with his. "O my boy, where have you been?"

"On the beach, O my chief, under the great canoe you once put in my care."

The king ran his rough hand over the boy's straight back. "Boy, what have you eaten?"

Ku suddenly smiled at his king. "Perhaps my chief recalls that I had bundles for the voyage. The dry food in the tree, left from the voyage, was my food."

The king called for his steward to bring fish and poi, and savory food, good things and fat things of the chief, for the boy to eat.

"Here I asked you to sail with me, and look how I rewarded you. But for you this traveler would not have returned. Boy, I thought you were with our people." Grief and shame brought more tears.

Ku ate in silence. He was hungry after the race; and how could he say to the grief of the king, 'It was not so.'? It was.

The king looked up, as if only then he recalled why the boy was there. "Boy, are you the one who raced a short time ago with my men?"

"'Ae, e ku'u ali'i. It was I."

"And you are the boy who raced today?"

"'Ae, e ku'u ali'i. It was I."

"What was the wager, boy?"

"In the first race, the fish were the wager, and I won. In this race, the men wished to wager the bones. I won, my chief. The imu heats on the beach and awaits them. The families weep a bundle of tears."

Keawe-nui-a-'Umi bowed his head, and his own tears gushed forth.

Ku asked softly, "Why these tears of the chief?"

"I weep for my men."

"O my chief, the wager was their wish, not mine. I had no wager; so I offered the canoe in my care as my wealth. They would not agree. They wished the bones. Because I had won their fish, they wished me to drink the bitter waters."

"My boy, your aloha for me once saved my life. If you still have aloha, I ask you to spare the lives of my men. They are not good at racing, but they are skilled fishermen. If they die, part of me dies with them."

"My chief, although I have reason to wish their death, I leave their life and death to you. But the servant asks his king, 'Do you think more of these men than of any other?'"

"I would not value them as I do, if I had found Paka'a. If Paka'a were here, I would not be neglected."

"O my chief, one bites into a fruit that is rotten. Wash the mouth, spit out the chewed part; in the mouth the bitterness sticks. If these men live, your servant Paka'a will not return."

The king looked sharply at Ku.

The boy went on. "O my chief, when Paka'a was with you, there were those who wished his power, his lands, his honor, even his place in your heart. They filled your ears with lies, and you listened. You pushed Paka'a from his canoes, from his place at court, from his place on the great canoe, from that place in your heart. Those who lied are no more and have gone the narrow stranded way, but the men they favored, who worked wrong against Paka'a, squat now on the sand and wait their end. Only you can give the word for Paka'a to return or not."

"Boy, if you know where he is, go and fetch Paka'a! Then these men will die."

"My chief, there was a storm at Moloka'i, and a boy warned his chief to come ashore."

"'Ae. I remember." Keawe-nui-a'Umi sat forward eagerly.

"My chief, the man with his head bent over his fish-line, who pretended to be deaf, that man was Paka'a."

"Auwe noho'i e! Is this right, boy?"

"My chief, the tale-bearing winds blow the cruel tales over and over, and cut the softness from a man's heart. That man is my father. And I am Ku-a-Paka'a, named for my grandfather and for the god who stands and does battle, but named also for the one my father loved above all, whose rough skin he did not wish to forget."

143

"Auwe!"

"Paka'a looked down; his heart was low that his king had lost faith in him. But he never lost aloha for his king."

"Auwe!"

"It was Paka'a who taught me the chants I know of the lands he loved. It was Paka'a who taught me the ways of the winds and the ways of the waters and how to find our way in them—to sail, to paddle, to fish. It was Paka'a who taught me to serve my king, to care for my king."

The old man sat as if under a spell at the boy's words. At last he bent his head and whispered, "Is this all true, my boy?"

" 'Ae, my chief. It is true. My father let me sail with you, because it was the only way his enemies might die and he be avenged. They died by their own will in the ocean in the face of all on the great canoe."

Keawe-nui-'Umi shook his head, afraid to believe, and fearful not to believe.

When Ku saw him waver, he said gently, "O my chief, do you recall when your malo was wet after the storm, I brought you a malo, I brought you a kapa to cover you in your coldness? Paka'a had told me to say they were mine. He wished not to be known until he could come back to his king with honor, free to stand head high in his place. For that, I did not give my name. But the malo and the kapa, O my chief, were yours."

Keawe-nui-a-'Umi faced truth. He wept aloud for Paka'a. He wept for his fishermen. But he gave the order for the men to be thrown in the imu they had made ready for Ku-a-Paka'a.

"My boy, sail at once to Moloka'i and tell Paka'a that those who wished him harm are dead. Tell him of my need for him. Tell him of my aloha for him."

"'Ae, e ku'u ali'i. I shall tell him."

The king ordered a canoe with a sail made ready, provisioned with poi and water, and bade paddlers go with the boy.

But Ku told his chief, "My chief, one adz carved the canoe of my father's plan. I am that adz. Alone I go, and I shall bring back Paka'a."

CHAPTER EIGHTEEN

Ku-a-Paka'a, son of chiefs, slept at court, and when dawn paled the eastern sky, took his calabash and went down to the beach. Boarding the canoe the king had ordered for him, he set up the sail, and the winds that bear the tales of the world, the trades, filled his sail and sent him on his way.

Ku made the lonely trip his father had made twelve years before, but the boy went in hope, hope for his father's return to his place, hope for his own future as son of chiefs. The arrows of a boy fly high, high over the brush and small rocks that make the old foot stumble. Ku had carried out the plan of his father. He had talked to the king at his court; and he knew now that as well as a god to be feared, a king was a man with a man's hungers, a man's tears, and could be weak as a man as well as strong. Might it not even be easier to love a man-king who falters than a god-king who cannot? Might there not be a better way to settle a wrong than to give weeping to a man's family?

The wind blew Ku's way; he had but to steer. Dawn flamed into daybreak. When the sun glitter broke through the eastern gate, Ku passed Maui. When the sun was high, he saw Moloka'i, and Ho'olehua, his land.

All the days since the boy had gone off with Keawe-nui-a-'Umi, Paka'a and Hikauhi followed their son in their hearts. Never had he been so far from them for so long.

The mother saw every wind stain on the waters a sail. Aloha filled her heart, and the fullness was pain and burst out into harsh words to who was nearest. Paka'a said nothing, but his eyes bored the horizon for a sign.

147

"Auwe! I long for the boy. You, Paka'a, let him go. Why did you not show yourself to your king? Your child might have lived."

Paka'a did not drop his eyes from where ocean meets sky. "The boy lives. He will come. I sent him to clear the way for us to hold the head high as once we did, in our own place. When my enemies have gone, then I can live in peace with my master."

Hikauhi said no more, knowing what sadness had carved the cheeks and sharpened the eyes of her husband. She stopped nagging and kept her longing to herself. But day after day she spent on a rise of ground where she could watch the waves beyond the reef.

One morning Paka'a saw a small canoe, far off, sailing out of the morning, a tern grazing the waves. He turned to Hikauhi: "Here comes our son. He is coming home!"

"Where? How do you know?"

"There. The feather on the water. I know. He comes from the east, from Hawai'i, from the king. My enemies are no more."

Hikauhi ran down to the beach. When the boy stood, he cast no shadow, but leaped onto the sand. Hikauhi ran to him and wept. She held his face in her hands and rubbed his nose with hers.

"Aloha! O my mother!"

And she who had had so many words before now had none at all.

Ku-a-Paka'a lifted his canoe up on the sand, took his paddle and calabash, and went up to the house where his father stood, his face sharp with waiting for the word. Paka'a opened his arms to the boy.

"How was your trip, my son?"

Ku smiled as he put the calabash of the winds into his father's hands.

"I was ready, O my father. You are avenged."

The big wave swamps even the strong canoe. Paka'a felt his heart almost go under in the flood of aloha for the boy and relief at his words. He held his son to him and wept.

When he had eaten, Ku-a-Paka'a told his father and mother of the trip, of the storm near Ka'ula, of the death of the two helmsmen in the sight of all, of the race for the fish, of the race for the bones. He told Paka'a he had talked to the king at his court as to a man.

"'Ae. He is a man," said Paka'a.

"E ku'u makuakane, he sent me to take you back. He said, 'Tell him his enemies are dead. Tell him of my need for him. Tell him of my aloha for him.' When shall we go?"

"What goods did your master give you?"

149

Ku looked surprised. "Nothing, Father. He asked me to fetch you."

"You asked him for nothing?"

Ku shook his head.

Paka'a looked down and spoke from the caution born of deep hurt. "My son, that was foolish. Canoes, a piece of land from the mountains to the sea, with these, one can be free, one can hold the head high. You must learn these things."

"Father, how could I know? I thought, the chief knows what a man is to him, he will reward the man."

"It seems so, my son. But a king can forget. Only when one is sure of one's place should one return to the court of a chief. Otherwise, better that I remain here on Moloka'i. Heaven curves above. Earth swings below. Here we can live and eat like chiefs."

"But here is the trouble, Father. The helmsmen, the fisherman have died. The king wept for you. His teeth are yellow, his eyes are blurred. He needs a strong backbone, Father. He needs you."

Paka'a looked off over the waters, as if he could see his chief...He then looked at Ku-a-Paka'a, whom he had taught in the ways of a backbone. "My son, go back to your master. Tell him Paka'a will come when his lands, his canoes, when all that he had, all that he was, are as they were before. We shall go to Hawai'i; we shall go in honor."

"'Ae, my father. When I have rested I shall set out."

Ku-a-Paka'a rested on Moloka'i for two days. On the third day, he made ready his canoe to sail back to Hawai'i.

CHAPTER NINETEEN

The day after Ku-a-Paka'a left Hawai'i for Moloka'i, Keawe-nui-a-'Umi watched the sea the day long for a sail in the west. He waited till dark, but the boy did not come. There was no sail, no Paka'a.

He sent for Kahiku-o-ka-moku. "Get a large canoe ready to sail to Moloka'i, to the boy's place. Ask there for Paka'a. The boy said he lives on Moloka'i and that he would bring him back to me. But he does not come."

"'Ae, my chief." Kahiku-o-ka-moku bade men rig a double canoe and get ready to sail in the morning. And one of the men he asked to go was Lapakahoe, half-brother of Paka'a.

151

In the early dawn of the third day, Kahiku-o-ka-moku and the paddlers boarded the canoe, put up the mast and sail, and set off for Moloka'i. When the sun was over their heads, they reached the land of the boy.

Ku-a-Paka'a had just finished checking his canoe lashings for the long paddle back to Hawai'i and was on his way to the house of his father when the people shouted, "There is a canoe!"

Paka'a saw the double canoe enter the harbor. "My son, here is one who looks for you. The chief sends for us. You stay here. I'll go to the house of your grandfather. In the evening we'll come."

Ku-a-Paka'a waited in his father's house until the visitors had lifted the canoe to dry land. Kahiku-o-ka-moku and the chiefs, his paddlers, came up to the house they knew from their stay before. Ku greeted them as a young chief greets his guests. He offered them food and mats for rest.

While they were resting, he asked, "You are bound where?"

"Here," said Kahiku-o-ka-moku.

"A trip for what purpose?"

"A trip to find Paka'a. The king has waited two days for you. He sent me to fetch the two of you." Kahiku-o-ka-moku studied the sure boy. Only a tall straight tree could put forth such a branch. "Boy, where is Paka'a?"

"I have not seen him because I expect a guest this evening. I await his arrival."

"When will that guest arrive?"

152

"He'll be here any time. He may be on his way now."

Before he took the visitors from Hawai'i to the mua to eat, Ku-a-Paka'a had sent word asking that Paka'a, Hikauhi, Ho'olehua, and Iloli and their people come with gifts. Kahiku-o-ka-moku and his companions must know that they were guests of the son of chiefs of Moloka'i of a long line.

While they waited for the guest, the people began to arrive with the gifts—kapa, potatoes, taro, fish, pigs, and dogs. First came the commoners and retainers. Then came Hikauhi, her brother Kaumanamana, Paka'a her husband, and last of all the high chiefs, Ho'olehua and Iloli.

"My guest comes!" cried Ku-a-Paka'a.·

Lapakahoe had been sitting facing the doorway of the house. When Paka'a stood in the doorway and Ku cried out, Lapakahoe stood up, calling out, "Here's Paka'a! Paka'a! O my brother!" He ran arms wide into the arms of his brother and friend, and they wept for aloha and joy.

Kahiku-o-ka-moku and the others from Hawai'i bounded to their feet and ran out of the house. When they saw that it truly was Paka'a they all wept and cried out, and the hard stone in Paka'a crumbled to feel their aloha.

The rest of the evening the guests and their hosts stretched out on the mats. Talk bubbled up and flowed, and many kukui nuts burned in the lamp. Kahiku-o-ka-moku told Paka'a all the boy had done for them once they had left Moloka'i.

"E Paka'a, why did you not show yourself to your

153

master? We almost died on that search for you. Our chief suffered the cold. But for your son, he would have gone back to Hawai'i a spirit."

"Someone said the calabash was broken, and it was put on the shelf. For a time two helmsmen were clever at steering their own futures. The stern of the great canoe, that never swamped when my paddle Lapakahoe steered, was taken from me and became the place of others."

"'Ae. You are right." The men were thoughtful. "But in that storm our chief cried out, 'My body would never be wet, were I with Paka'a!'"

"I did not wish my chief to know me until my way back to him was clear."

"And the boy who sailed with us is your son?"

"'Ae. My son, who avenged me." Paka'a presented Hikauhi to the others. "This is the mother of the boy, my wife, who wed me, a stranger to this land of Moloka'i."

"You will come back with us to Hawai'i? The king, your adopted child, asks it of you."

"If I am once more helmsmen for my chief, if all my lands, all my canoes that were taken from me, are mine once more, if my place is as it was, then I shall go back. You, Kahiku-o-ka-moku, take the boy with you and go back to our chief. When our master gives me his word, then you may come for me and mine."

"'Ae." Kahiku-o-ka-moku was relieved. Once more the kingly house would have a pillar.

At dawn the next morning the men readied the canoe. Paka'a brought rich food gifts for Keawe-nui-a-'Umi. He put into the hands of Ku-a-Paka'a the king's malo, the king's kapas, so that the king should know that it was truly Paka'a who had sent them. Kahiku-o-ka-moku and Ku-a-Paka'a boarded the double canoe, and they set sail for Hawai'i.

CHAPTER TWENTY

By afternoon the double canoe arrived at Kawaihae. Kahiku-o-ka-moku ordered the gifts from Paka'a to be taken to the court. Then he and Ku-a-Paka'a went before the king.

"Did you find Paka'a?"

"'Ae. We found him, O my chief," said Kahiku-o-ka-moku. "He sent you these kapas, this malo, so that you would know it was surely he."

Keawe-nui-a-'Umi looked at the kapas that Ku held out to him. "'Ae. These are my kapas. But where then is Paka'a?"

"My chief, Paka'a stays on Moloka'i until his chief sends word that all his lands, all his canoes, his honor and his place, will be as once they were. If you give this word, O my chief, I shall fetch him. He will come."

"Auwe! The paddler too hasty loses the race. I sent for the backbone but forgot the man. Sail again to Moloka'i and give him my word that I agree to all he asks. To bring back Paka'a and his, tax the people canoes to number five forties. A fleet to cloud the waters will tell him and his people my aloha for him. The boy will stay here with us."

In a few days the fleet of canoes had gathered at Kawaihae.

One day as Paka'a gazed over the sea between Maui and Moloka'i, he saw a fleet of canoes like a school of flying fish, sending the spray flying, raising a mist over the waters.

156

He called to Hikauhi, "They come to take us to Hawai'i!"

"O my husband, let us go." By the cloud of canoes on the waters, the wife learned of her husband's place in his own land. "There we shall live as chiefs."

"'Ae. But my thought is that you lived with me when I came here a stranger. I do not forget that, Hikauhi."

With a flash and a swish of paddles the canoes sailed through the surf and landed on the sand at Kaluako'i. Kahiku-o-ka-moku ran up to find Paka'a. "The chief sends his word. He agrees to all his servant asks."

157

"Then let us go to Hawai'i!"

Paka'a asked his family, his followers, and any who wished to go with him as retainers to get ready. Five forties of canoes could hardly hold the people who wished to go to Hawai'i as followers of Paka'a.

As they neared the big island, the eyes of Paka'a glittered as he saw once more his land, and the head of Mauna Kea rise from its lei of clouds. When the fleet swept in to shore at Kawaihae, the people on the beach rushed toward the water with chants, with leis of leaves. The last double canoe bore Kahiku-o-ka-moku, Hikauhi, and Paka'a.

"Here is Paka'a! He comes home!"

When they landed, Paka'a, in the helmet and mantle of a chief, went before his king. By the side of Keawe-nui-a-'Umi stood Ku-a-Paka'a, wearing the kapa and malo of the son of a chief and bearing the kahili of the king.

Keawe-nui-a-'Umi rose and hurried to embrace Paka'a. As the king wept for shame at his treatment of his friend and backbone, as he wept for joy for the friend's return, Ku saw the tears pour down the furrows in his father's face.

After the storm the white water pours down the clefts in the hills, where the rain and the adz-wind have worn away the softness, the yielding, have left the knife-like folds of heart rock. Then the sun bursts through the black cloud, the light glistens on the spears of lauhala, on the pale green of the kukui, the mists float off the cliffs as veils of fine kapa. And the wind creatures whose home is the air wheel in for shelter in the deep clefts of that heart rock.

Ku looked up at the kahili he held—the flare and spread of the feathers of the red 'i'iwi that drinks honey from Pele's flower, the sacred lehua; the white human bone honored to be set in the hardwood shaft; the pure white kapa streamer. The kahili to hold over a king as he wakes and as he sleeps, to protect him, to sign his place, to mark his pride.

When the time of strangeness between Paka'a and Keawe-nui-a-'Umi was over, each told the other what had passed, and they lived in peace.

Paka'a took up once more the king's kahili, the carved 'awa bowl, the great steering paddle. Once more he was an honored chief of great bundles and many lands. Ku-a-Paka'a was in his rightful place, where he would grow strong, in his time a backbone, Ku, son of Paka'a.

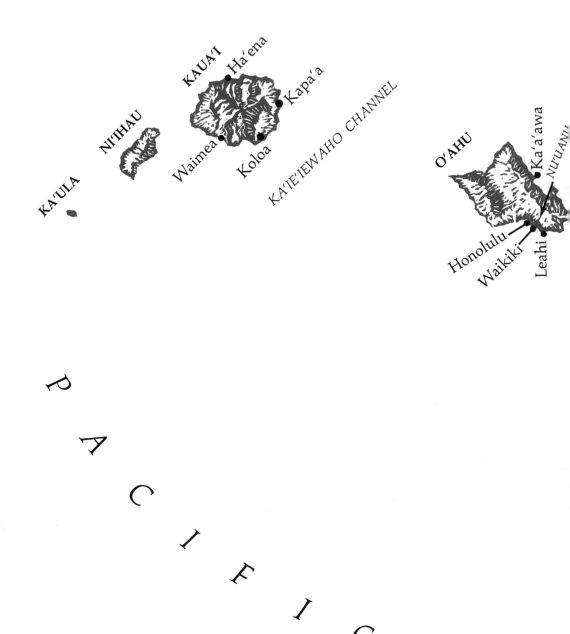

KAUA'I

Ha'ena

Kapa'a

NI'IHAU

Waimea

Koloa

KA'IE'IEWAHO CHANNEL

KA'ULA

O'AHU

Ka'a'awa

NU'ULANU

Honolulu

Waikiki

Leahi

P A C I F I C

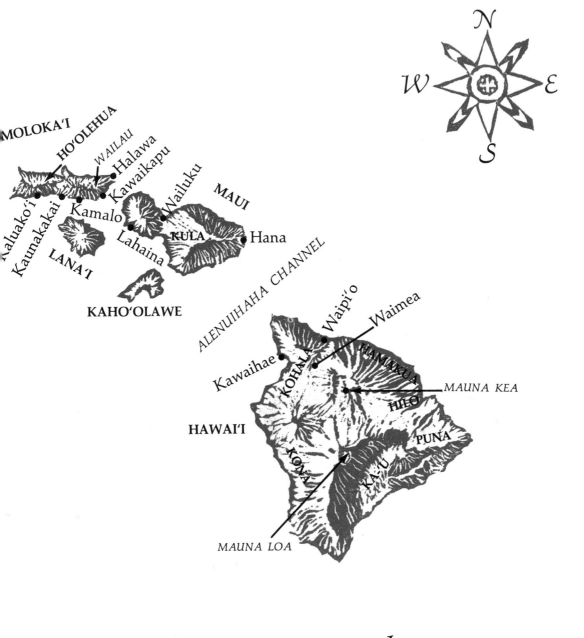

N

W   E

S

MOLOKA'I

HO'OLEHUA

WAILAU

Halawa

Kawaikapu

Kaluako'i

Kaunakakai   Kamalo

Wailuku

MAUI

LANA'I

Lahaina

KULA

Hana

KAHO'OLAWE

ALENUIHAHA CHANNEL

Waipi'o   Waimea

Kawaihae

KOHALA

HAMAKUA

HILO

MAUNA KEA

HAWAI'I

PUNA

KONA

KA'U

MAUNA LOA

O   C   E   A   N

Many Hawaiian proper names have meaning in themselves; many are combinations of other words. Since the ancient Hawaiians had no written language, some of these meanings have passed out of memory and become lost, as have the exact locations of some of the place names mentioned in the old chants. Extraordinarily sensitive to every nuance of changes in nature, the Hawaiians gave names to well over a hundred of the winds that breathed on or swept over their islands; they named individual mountains and cliffs, often even large rocks. While the same name may have occurred on several of the islands, in general those locations given here are the ones used in the story. The parts of some long proper names have been separated by hyphens to aid pronunciation.

The Hawaiian alphabet is composed of thirteen letters: the vowels, *a, e, i, o, u;* the consonants, *h, k, l, m, n, p, w;* and the glottal break, represented by ('). The glottal break represents the Polynesian *k,* attenuated until almost elided; it is similar to the break between vowels in a fast pronunciation of *oh-oh.*

The vowels are generally similar in sound to those in Italian: long *a* (ā) or stressed *a* (a•) as in *father;* unstressed *a* as in *above;* long *e* (ē) or stressed *e* (e•) as in *obey;* unstressed *e* as in *bet;* long *i* (ī) or stressed *i* (i•) as in *marine;* unstressed *i* as in *it;* long *o* (ō) or stressed *o* (o•) as in *rose;* unstressed *o* as in *democrat;* long *u* (ū) or stressed *u* (u•) as in *rule;* unstressed *u* as in *pull.*

After *o* and *u, w* is pronounced as *w,* as in *Auwe!* After *i* and *e, w* is usually pronounced as *v.* After *a,* and initially it may be pronounced as either *w* or *v.*

Combined vowel sounds begin with a stress on the first letter and end in a sound similar to that of the vowel ending the diphthong:

ai and *ae,* like English *i* in *line,* closing to *i* and *e,* respectively;
ao and *au,* like *ow* in *how,* closing to *o* or *u;*
ei, like English *a* in *lay;*
oe and *oi,* as in *oil,* closing to *e* or *i;*
ou, like *o* in *vote,* closing to *u;*
oa, as *oah* in *Noah.*

165

All syllables end in a vowel; all long vowels are stressed. Otherwise stress is usually on the next to the last syllable and on alternating preceding syllables. Stresses are indicated here by periods (·).

'ae ('ae)   yes; expression of agreement.

ala (a·la)   wake up.

Alenuihaha (a·le nu·i ha·ha)
   proud wave; channel between islands of Maui and Hawai'i.

ali'i (a li· 'i)
   a chief; a king; one who rules or has the right to rule over other men.

aloha (a lo·ha)   love; sympathy.

aloha 'ino! (a lo·ha 'i·no)
   How dreadful! Expression of intense pity for one suffering.

aloha nui loa (a lo·ha nu·i lo·a)
   very great love.

Aluli ('ā· lu li)
   inclined head; possibly a mountain on Moloka'i.

'a'ole ('a 'o·le)   no; not.

'A'ole loa! ('a 'o·le lo·a)
   Certainly not! I should say not!

Auwe! (au wē·)
   Alas! Oh! Too bad! An exclamation of emotion: wonder, surprise, fear, pity, etc.

Auwe noho'i e! (au wē· no ho·'i e·)
   Oh, my goodness! Emphatic form of Auwe!

'awa ('a·wa)
   a mild narcotic drink made from the root of *Piper methysticum*.

e (e)   call for attention.

E ala! (e· a·la)   Arise! Wake up!

'Ehu ('e·hu)   redheaded; name of a chief of Kona.

166

ei nei ('ei• nei•)

    you there; the one here. Said to one person, usually someone close to the speaker.

'elepaio ('e•le pai•o)

    type of woodpecker or flycatcher (*Chasiempsis sandwichensis sandwichensis*); an aspect of the goddess Lea. The bird's pecking on tree trunks showed that the wood was unsound for canoe-making.

Ha'ena (hā•'e•na)

    burning red; point on northern coast of island of Kaua'i where sunset is often red.

haku (ha•ku)

    to weave; to compose; to put in order; lord; master.

haku mele (ha•ku me•le)   composers of chants, or poets.

hala (ha•la)

    screwpine (*Pandanus odoratissimus*), a small tree which suggests a palm. The leaves were stripped of their thorns and woven into mats, or used as thatch. The fruit was used for leis and for paint-brushes.

Halawa (hā•la•wa)

    curve; deep valley and cape on the northeastern tip of the island of Moloka'i.

Hamakua (hā•mā•ku•a)

    a district of land on the northeastern side of the island of Hawai'i.

Hana (ha•na)

    bay, valley (only in place names, as Hanalei; also Hono–,as in Honolulu); place on eastern part of island of Maui.

hau (hau)

    lowland tree of hibiscus family (*Hibiscus tiliaceus*), with yellow flowers; used medicinally. Curving branches were used for out-riggers for canoes; the bast was used for rope.

167

Hawaiʻi (ha waiꞏʻi)
>   both the farthest eastern island and the group of islands of the Hawaiian chain.

heiau (heiꞏau)   temple; place of worship.

Hikauhi (hi kauꞏhi)
>   of no use; without profit or result; name of wife of Pakaʻa. (Word came from the saying *Hikauhi i Kaumanamana*. A woman, Hikauhi, disappeared just before giving birth, and her husband searched for her in vain. An unpleasant name was often given to a child to fend off evil spirits.)

Hilo (hiꞏlo)
>   name of famous Polynesian navigator; place on eastern part of island of Hawaiʻi, famous for rain.

hinalea (hiꞏna leꞏa)
>   a fish, one of small-to-moderate-sized, brightly colored wrasses (family *Labridae*). Eaten as an aftertaste after drinking ʻawa.

Hololua (hoꞏlo luꞏa)
>   to run, sail, move in two directions; place on Maui, possibly named because the wind blows in two directions.

Honolulu (hoꞏno luꞏlu)
>   calm bay; place on southern shore of island of Oʻahu where an opening in the coral reef made a calm bay. (Formerly called Kou.)

Hoʻokele-i-Hilo (hoꞏʻo keꞏle i hiꞏlo)
>   Steer-to-Hilo, name of a helmsman of the king of Hawaiʻi. (hoʻokele: to navigate, to steer.)

Hoʻokele-i-Puna (hoꞏʻo keꞏle i puꞏna)
>   Steer-to-Puna, name of a helmsman of the king of Hawaiʻi.

Hoʻolehua (hōꞏʻo le huꞏa)
>   swift, strong; name of a chief of Molokaʻi; place name, west central part of Molokaʻi.

hoʻopi (hoꞏʻo pǐꞏ)   stingy, frugal.

Hua'a (hu.a 'ā.)

> very sour (of poi); possibly a person of sour disposition; name of a chief of Puna.

hula (hu.la)   the dance; to move to rhythmic song or chant.

'ie'ie ('i.e 'i.e)

> woody, branching climber (*Freycinetia arborea*), growing in forests at 1500 feet.

'i'iwi ('i 'i.wi)

> native bird, the scarlet honey creeper (*Vestiaria coccinea*), found on all the main islands of Hawai'i.

'ilima ('i li.ma)

> shrub (*Sida fallax*), used medicinally. Flowers were used for royal leis, only chiefs being allowed to wear them.

Iloli (ī.lo.li)

> a strong odor; a chiefess of Moloka'i, mother of Hikauhi; western section of Moloka'i, near Ho'olehua.

imu (I.mu)   roasting oven in ground.

'iwa ('i.wa)   the frigate bird (*Fregata minor palmerstoni*).

Ka'a'awa (ka.'a 'a.wa)

> ka'a: to roll; 'awa: mist, cold mountain rain; place on windward O'ahu, name possibly referring to rolling mist.

ka'au (ka.'au)

> forty; Hawaiians counted by fours. Two ka'au were eighty.

kahala (ka ha.la)

> the amberjack, a food fish (*Seriola spp.*); also a proper name.

Kahiku-o-ka-moku (ka hi.ku o ka mo.ku)

> the seventh island; name of a powerful officer of the high chief Keawe-nui-a-'Umi.

kahili (ka hi.li)

> the feather standard of royalty; a fly whisk.

Kahoʻolawe (ka ho•ʻo la•we)
   a subtraction; an island to the south of Maui, thought to have
   been at one time a part of Maui.

kahu (ka•hu)   guardian; keeper.

kahu iwikuamoʻo (ka•hu i•wi ku•a mo•ʻo)
   royal guardian; backbone (fig.); a chief's near relative and personal attendant.

Kahuku (ka hu•ku)
   lump, protuberance; name of a jutting promontory on northern-
   most part of island of Oʻahu.

kahuna (ka hu•na)
   an expert in any specialized line; usually a priest.

Kaʻieʻiewaho (ka ʻi•e ʻi•e wa•ho)
   channel between Oʻahu and Kauaʻi.

Kaʻili (kā•ʻi•li)
   to snatch; red feather god of ʻUmi line of chiefs. At a later date
   the image was called Ku-Kaʻili-moku: Ku, the island snatcher.

Kailua (kai lu•a)
   turbulent sea; place on southeastern coast of island of Oʻahu.

Kainui (kai nu•i)
   great sea current; probably referred to a place on coast of
   Molokaʻi.

Kalihi (ka li•hi)
   edge; land division west of Honolulu on island of Oʻahu.

Kaluakoʻi (ka lu•a ko•ʻi)
   adz pit or quarry; place name on southern Molokaʻi.

Kamalo (ka•ma lo•)
   arid; place name on southern shore of Molokaʻi.

Kamaʻoa (ka mā•ʻo• a)
   place in Ka-ʻu, southwestern district of the island of Hawaiʻi.

Kanaloa (ka•na lo•a)

> god of the ocean and of all things within it; god of healing; one of the four major Hawaiian gods, called Tangaroa in southern Polynesia.

Kane (ka•ne)

> god of beauty, life, creation, with many aspects; one of the four major Hawaiian gods.

kapa (ka•pa)

> cloth beaten from bark, especially of the wauke or paper mulberry (Broussonetia papyrifera), or the mamaki (Pipturus albidus); used for clothing, bed clothes, etc.

Kapa'a (ka pa•'a)

> steadfast; fixed; place on eastern shore of Kaua'i.

kapu (ka•pu)

> forbidden, or sacred; a prohibition; a special privilege or exemption from ordinary taboo. The kapu of the dead refers to the days devoted to rituals for the burial and mourning of the dead.

Kapukini (ka•pu ki•ni)

> multitude of kapus; name of a chiefess of Hawai'i, the mother of Keawe-nui-a-'Umi, and sister and wife of Liloa.

Ka-'u (ka 'ū•)

> the breast; name of southwestern district of the island of Hawai'i, named for the mother mountain, Mauna Loa.

Kaua'i (kau a•'i)   name of one of the Hawaiian islands.

Ka'ula (ka 'u•la)

> a sea bird; name of an islet off Ni'ihau, to the west of Kaua'i, so far to the west that often the expression "to be on Ka'ula" meant to be dead.

Kaulua (kau lu•a)

> of two minds; last month of the Hawaiian year, corresponding to February in some localities, often a month of alternating cool and warm spells and rough weather.

Kaumanamana (kau ma·na ma·na)
branching; name of brother of Hikauhi; place name on southwestern Moloka'i.

Kaunakakai (kau·na ka kai·)
net for hanging a calabash; place name on southern shore of Moloka'i.

Kawaihae (ka wai·hae·)
raging water; place in Kohala, on the northwest shore of the island of Hawai'i.

Kawaikapu (ka wai·ka·pu)
sacred water; place name on southeastern Moloka'i.

Keawe-nui-a-'Umi (ke a·we nu·i a 'u·mi)
Great Keawe, son of 'Umi; a high chief of the island of Hawai'i.

keiki (kei·ki)   child; son. (ke keiki: the child).

Kiauau (kī·au au)   Hurry!

Kiholo (kī·ho·lo)
large wooden fishhook; a large fishnet; name of a small bay below Kawaihae on northwest coast of the island of Hawai'i.

koa (ko·a)
largest of native forest trees *(Acacia koa)*, growing to one hundred feet, with leaves a pale greyish green; a hard wood.

koali (ko a·li)
a morning glory *(Ipomoea congesta)*. The vines were used for swings and nets.

Kohala (ko ha·la)
name of the northwestern district of the island of Hawai'i.

kolea (kō·le a)
Pacific golden plover *(Pluviolis dominica fulvus)*. The bird summers in Alaska and Siberia for breeding and winters in Hawai'i and New Zealand.

172

Koloa (kō·lo a)
Tall cane; name of a district on southeastern Kaua'i.

Kona (ko•na)

   southwest; name of leeward wind; name of a district on the western part of the island of Hawai'i; leeward side of any island in
   the group.

Ku (ku)

   one of the four major Hawaiian gods, said to be a god of war, and
   in Hawai'i, a god of canoes.

Kuaiwa (ku•a i•wa)

   handsome back; probably a place name on Maui or Moloka'i.

Kualoa (ku•a lo•a)

   long back; a mountain and land area on the eastern coast of O'ahu,
   a site for squidding.

Ku-a-Nu'uanu (ku•a nu•'u a•nu)

   Ku, son of Nu'uanu (cool heights); name of the father of Paka'a.

Ku-a-Paka'a (ku•a pā•ka•'a)   Ku, son of Paka'a.

kukui (ku ku•i)

   the candlenut tree (*Aleurites moluccana*), extremely important to
   the Hawaiians. The nuts were used as torches, as lamps when
   strung on the midrib of a coconut leaf, as seasoning, medicinally
   as a purgative, and for making necklaces. Chewed nuts spat on
   rough water calmed areas for fishing. The soft wood was used for
   making canoes, the nut coats and roots for making a black dye, the
   gum from the bark for painting kapa, the leaves for polishing the
   nuts.

Kula (ku•la)

   plain; open country; name of a district on eastern Maui.

Kulukulu'a (ku•lu ku•lu 'ā•)

   sap from green kukui nuts, used as an antiseptic for cuts and as a
   gargle for sore throats; name of a legendary chief of Hilo.

Kumukahi (ku•mu ka•hi)

   origin; beginning; a point on the southeastern tip of the island of
   Hawai'i.

Kupeke (ku pe•ke)
to halt and take short steps; place name on southeastern Moloka'i.

ku'u (ku•'u)   my. (Ku'u haku! Ku'u ali'i! My lord! My chief!)

La'a (la•'a)   sacred; dedicated. Possibly refers to Laka.

La'amaomao (la•'a mao•mao•)
distant sacred one; goddess of the winds.

Lahaina (la hai•na)
possibly, cruel sun; name of northwestern district of Maui.

Laka (la•ka)   goddess of the hula.

Lapakahoe (la•pa ka ho•e)
Flash-of-the-paddle; name of younger half-brother of Paka'a.

lauhala (lau ha•la)
leaves of the hala. Dried and prepared leaves were used for making mats, baskets, etc.

Lea (le•a)
wife of the god Ku; goddess of canoe builders, sometimes taking
form of elepaio woodpecker.

Leahi (le a•hi)
name of extinct volcanic crater overlooking Waikiki on the island
of O'ahu; later called Diamond Head.

lehua (le hu•a)
the bright red flower of the 'ohi'a lehua (Metrosideros collina), a
large tree of the cool uplands with hard dark wood. The flowers
were sacred to Pele, legendary goddess of the volcano.

lei (lei)   necklace; wreath; garland.

Liloa (li lo•a)
name of early Hawaiian chief, father of 'Umi; possibly a former
place name on Maui.

Limahuli (li•ma hu•li)
curled fist; place name on the northern coast of Kaua'i, near
Ha'ena.

Lono (lo•no)
>   one of the four major Hawaiian gods; god of rain, fertility, agriculture, peace, family worship, weather phenomena.

Mahalo nui (mā•ha•lo nu•i)
>   thank you very much; many thanks.

maile (mai•le)
>   twining shrub *(Alyxia olivaeformis)* with fragrant leaves, growing in the cool, deep forests; made into open garlands worn by Hawaiian chiefs and commoners.

Maʻilou (ma•ʻi lou•)   name of uncle of Pakaʻa.

Makaha (mā•ka ha)
>   fierce; savage; name of a chief of the district of Ka-ʻu on the island of Hawaiʻi.

Makaluhau (ma•ka lū•hau)
>   dewy eyes; place name on Molokaʻi.

makuahine (ma ku•a hi•ne)
>   mother; female parent; not used alone in polite address (E kuʻu makuahine: Say, my mother...).

makuakane (ma ku•a ka•ne)
>   father, male parent; not used alone in polite address. (E kuʻu makuakane: Say, my father...).

Malama (ma la•ma)
>   month; light; place name on southeastern Hawaiʻi.

malo (ma•lo)
>   loincloth of kapa, in width nine to ten inches, in length three to four yards. The loincloth of a chief was held to be sacred.

malolo (mā•lo lo)   flying fish.

mana (ma•na)   might; supernatural or divine power.

manini (ma ni•ni)
>   surgeon fish, the convict tang, found on the reef.

Maui (mau•i)

  name of famous demi-god and trickster who snared the sun and discovered fire; name of one of the Hawaiian islands.

Mauna Kea (mau•na ke•a)

  white mountain; highest mountain in the Hawaiian islands, 13,796 ft. above sea level, on the island of Hawai'i. The summit of Mauna Kea is often snow-covered.

mele (me•le)   chant; poem.

moi (moi)

  threadfish, much esteemed for food. A large school of moi was an omen of disaster for chiefs.

Moloka'i (mo lo ka•'i)

  name of one of the Hawaiian islands.

mua (mu•a)

  men's eating house, kapu to women. Men and women ate separately.

Napu'u (nā•pu•'u)

  the hills; place in the district of Kona, western part of island of Hawai'i.

na'u (nā•'ū•)

  mine; for me. Children of Kona would make a prolonged u-sound just at sunset, believing that the sun would not set as long as they held the sound without taking a breath.

Nihoa (ni ho•a)

  toothed rocks; place name on Moloka'i where walls were built with jagged rocks.

nui (nu•i)   great; large.

Nu'uanu (nu•'u a•nu)

  cool heights; a high valley and pass on O'ahu.

O'ahu (o 'a•hu)   name of one of the Hawaiian islands.

'oia ('oi•a)   right; yes; it is so; go ahead.

Ola (o•la)   life; health; name of legendary chief of Kaua'i.

'olapa (ō•la pa)   a tree with fragrant leaves (*Cheirodendron*).

olona (o lo nā•)
    shrub (*Touchardia latifolia*) with strong fibers in the bark, used
    for making strong ropes, fishlines, and cords.

'opelu ('ō•pe lu)   mackerel (*Decapterus pinnulatus*).

'O'u-holowai-o-La'a ('ō•'ū• ho•lo wai• o la•'a)
    a kapa associated with the goddess Laka, said to be made at Ola'a
    (also La'a), in Puna on the island of Hawai'i.

pa (pā)   fence; royal enclosure; pen; house yard.

pahu hula (pa•hu hu•la)
    large drum made of a section of a coconut trunk with a sharkskin
    head, used to accompany the hula.

Pai'ea (pai•'e a)   edible crab; name of a chief of Kaua'i.

Paka'a (pā•ka•'a)
    skin cracked from drinking 'awa; name of legendary royal guard-
    ian of Keawe-nui-a-'Umi.

Pala'au (pā•lā•'au)
    wooden fence; name of suitor of Hikauhi; place name on northern
    Moloka'i.

pali (pa•li)   cliff; precipice; steep hill.

pau (pau)   finished; complete.

Pele (pe•le)   goddess of the volcano and of fire.

Pikoi-a-ka-'alala (pī•koi a• ka 'a la lā•)   Pikoi, son of the crow.

pili (pi•li)
    a type of grass used for thatch (*Heteropon contortus*)

poi (poi)
    paste made by pounding cooked taro root and water, a main article
    of food of the Hawaiians. It could also be made from sweet potato,
    breadfruit, banana.

pola (po•la)

platform or high seat between the two hulls of a double canoe.

Pueo-hulu-nui (pu e•o hu•lu nu•i)

owl with many feathers; the Hawaiian short-eared owl (*Asio flammeus sandwichensis*).

pulo'ulo'u (pū•lo•'u lo•'u)

white kapa ball on standard used as insignia of kapu.

Puna (pu•na)

spring of water; name of southeastern district of island of Hawai'i, famed for fragrance of hala.

taro (ta•ro) or **kalo** (ka•lo)

a kind of aroid (*Colocasia esculenta*) cultivated since ancient times for food, spreading from the tropics of the Old World. The leaves are eaten as lu-au, the starchy root as poi.

ti (tī) or **ki** (kī)

plant with shiny, long leaves, member of the lily family (*Cordyline terminalis*), used for wrapping food, for making raincapes, sandals, thatch, and as a protection against evil.

Ua kulu ka po! (u•a ku•lu ka po•)   The night is spent!

uhu (u•hu)

parrot fish (of which *Scarus perspicillatus* is most abundant and the largest), plant eaters, with strong, beak-like teeth for clipping food off coral.

Ukoa (u ko•a)

place name on northwestern O'ahu, near Haleiwa; possibly a place on Kaua'i with a strong wind.

'Umi ('u•mi)

name of early king of Hawai'i; father of Keawe-nui-a-'Umi.

uoa (u o•a)

a silvery food fish (*Neomyxus chaptalii*), known as false mullet.

Wa'ahila (wa•'a hi•la)   place name, probably on Kaua'i or Ka'ula.

Wahilani   (wa•hi la•ni)

    heavenly place; name of a chief of Kohala, a district on the island of Hawaiʻi.

Waiakea   (wai•a ke•a)

    a type of taro; place name in Hilo area on the island of Hawaiʻi.

Waialaʻe   (wai•a la•ʻe)

    water frequented by mudhens; place name on southeastern Oʻahu.

Waikiki   (wai ki kī•)

    spurting or rapid water; section of southern Oʻahu near Honolulu, formerly a residence of high chiefs of Oʻahu.

Wailau   (wai•lau•)

    branching waters; name of a valley on northeast Molokaʻi, famous for large bundles of food wrapped in leaves.

Wailuku   (wai lu•ku)

    destructive water; place name on northwestern Maui.

Waimea   (wai me•a)

    reddish water; name of western district of Kauaʻi; place name in Kohala on northwestern Hawaiʻi.

Waipiʻo   (wai pi•ʻo)

    arched water; rainbow; name of valley on windward coast of island of Hawaiʻi.

Wanuʻa   (wā•nuʻa)

    time of lush growth; name of chief of the district of Hamakua on the island of Hawaiʻi.

SOME ENGLISH EXPRESSIONS EXPLAINED

black sands   crushed lava sand from volcanic eruptions.

Bright One, the Sky God

    Wakea; noon; the sun; the light of day. Hawaiian high chiefs were believed to have been descended from the gods.

calabash

> a gourd or carved wooden bowl-like container, used for holding poi, water, fishnets, clothing; used for storage and for serving some types of food.

days of Ku

> days of the Ku taboo, the third, fourth, fifth, and sixth days of the lunar month, originally spent by the chiefs at the temple in prayer. Hawaiians had names for the days of the month but none for the days of the week.

gods

> The four major Hawaiian gods, all male deities, were Ku, Kane, Lono, and Kanaloa, and were worshipped by chiefs and commoners alike, often in different aspects. There were also various female gods and a countless multitude of spirits and lesser deities.

great star of Kane   a Hawaiian term for the sun.

lei of stars   the Pleides or small eyes.

rainbow

> thought to be the sign of the presence of a high chief.

red star   probably Sirius.

sennit

> coconut fiber braided and used for lashings, cordage.

string game

> hei, a type of cat's cradle game with many figures, a game at which Hawaiians excelled, being expert riggers.

whale-tooth necklace

> the lei palaoa, a necklace of braided human hair with a carved whale tooth pendant, a symbol of power and menace, and regarded as the exclusive property of chiefs.